In THE WATCH BELOW, James White's remarkable talent for extrapolating human survival under enormously hostile conditions is exploited to the full in a tense and moving novel of a group of humans trapped in the hull of a sunken ship—for generations!

Skilfully woven into the desperate problems which confront the handful of men and women is the story of a far different group of beings, creatures who face extermination with courage and determination equal to that of the humans—a parallel saga of sweep and power and breathtaking suspense!

Also by James White

LIFEBOAT
THE ALIENS AMONG US
ALL JUDGMENT FLED
DEADLY LITTER
MAJOR OPERATION
STAR SURGEON
TOMORROW IS TOO FAR
HOSPITAL STATION

Published by Ballantine Books

THE
WATCH
BELOW

James White

BALLANTINE BOOKS • NEW YORK

To
JOHN CARNELL

Friend, Agent, Slave-driver

With Thanks

Copyright © 1966 by James White

All rights reserved

SBN 345-02795-7-095

First Printing: February, 1966
Second Printing: August, 1972

Printed in the United States of America

Cover art by Dean Ellis

BALLANTINE BOOKS, INC.
101 Fifth Avenue, New York, N.Y. 10003
An Intext Publisher

I

From space the Earth was a serene and beautiful world circling a young and relatively cool sun. The great ice caps, the tremendous stretches of ocean, and the dazzling white carpets of the cloud layers were blurred both by distance and atmospheric haze, so that outwardly it was a planet of great beauty and peace. It would have required a telescope of fantastic power and definition to resolve the tiny sparks on the night side which were torpedoed ships or bombed and burning towns, and on the sunlit hemisphere the disturbances caused by the waging of World War Two were also of too minor a nature to register over interstellar distances.

It was February 3, 1942. . . .

Eleven days out of St. Johns, its ranks thinned to begin with by the unceasing attacks of the wolf packs and then scattered in disorder by a storm which was bad even for the North Atlantic in winter, the remnants of Convoy RK47 were in the process of reforming in the area of Rockall Deep prior to entering the relative safety of the Irish Sea. Most of the ships were within sight of a few others, but there were lone stragglers as well, and one which apparently had the ocean all to itself was the converted tanker *Gulf Trader*.

The *Trader* was unusual in that she was an oil tanker not carrying oil. Originally designed as a fleet oiler for the United States Navy, and then converted to commercial operation between the Gulf of Mexico and South America because the powers-that-were had thought that the world in 1938 was too peaceful a place for the Navy to need another fleet auxiliary, she was now in the process of being converted into something which might be an answer to the U-boat menace. There was no certainty about this, of

5

course, but any idea which might conceivably help against the wolf packs had to be tried.

For behind *Gulf Trader* lay the memory of five sinkings. One, a sister tanker, had vomited blazing fuel over half a mile of sea before going down and leaving a torch in the wake of the convoy which had burned all that night. And there was the munitions ship which had gone so suddenly that seconds later all that was left was a blotchy green afterimage of the flash and the dying echoes of that savage, crashing detonation. The other ships had died less dramatically, with the sounds of the explosions lost in the screaming wind and the blazing upperworks seen only as a dull glow through the driving snow and spray. Despite the long dogleg to the north the convoy had not been able to shake off the wolf packs. Only the storm had been able to achieve that feat, forcing them to seek shelter in the depths where their fragile pressure hulls would be safe from the hurtling mountains and avalanches of water above.

But now, after five raging days of it, the storm was dying. The sky had cleared and the sun was melting the unnatural streamlining of frozen spray and snow from *Trader's* superstructure. The sea was still mountainous, but its slopes were smooth now and the valleys were no longer filled with spray. Yet, the improving conditions meant that enemy reconnaissance aircraft would be seeking out the scattered convoy and directing their U-boats towards it, and that Allied aircraft would be spotting and, where possible, trying to sink the enemy submarines.

In the wheelhouse of *Gulf Trader* Captain Larmer sagged a little more heavily against the strap which, except for a number of unavoidable absences totaling not more than two hours, had held him in an upright if not always wakeful position on his stool for the past three days. He was looking at the signal which had just been handed to him and, although the words were printed boldly and legibly, for some reason their meaning was taking a long time to reach his brain. It was as if fatigue had surrounded him with a thick, invisible cocoon which slowed and deadened everything trying to pass through it, but finally the marks on the flimsy surrendered their meaning and

6

Larmer said, "Two subs have been reported in this area. How about that! We're advised to maintain maximum vigilance and proceed with caution!"

Beside him Lieutenant Commander Wallis nodded stiffly but did not speak.

There were times, Larmer thought tiredly, when trying to be pleasant to Wallis hardly seemed worth the effort. Anyone would think that Captain Larmer was going to take over the ship from Wallis when they reached Liverpool instead of vice versa. Between the storm and the U-boats it had been a very unpleasant trip, and the presence of the Royal Navy on board had not added to the social atmosphere of the ship.

Traditionally there had always been a certain difference of opinion between the merchant service and the Navy proper, for having to work harder under much stricter discipline for less pay it was natural that the Naval ratings felt superior to their sloppily dressed and overpaid colleagues. The filthy weather, the general tension, and the chronic lack of proper rest all played their part in aggravating the situation. At the same time Larmer was sure that the ratings engaged in modifying the tanks could have tried a little harder to conceal their feelings of superiority, that his own chief and the engineer lieutenant who was familiarizing himself with *Trader's* engine room could have conversed without giving the impression that they were on the point of committing mutual and bloody murder, and that the lieutenant commander could speak just a few words which were not shop. So far as Larmer could see the only exception among the Naval types was Radford, the surgeon lieutenant who was to be attached to the ship when she became H.M.S. something-or-other. Radford was not a very friendly type either, but he had been kept too busy in his professional capacity during this trip to arouse anything but admiration. This train of thought brought him back to the signal in his hand and the few hopelessly inadequate precautions he could take regarding it.

He said, "I hate to break up the party that Dickson and your doctor must be having with those girls, but under the circumstances it might be better if we moved them up

7

top. What I mean is, they've been torpedoed once this trip already. . . ."

While Larmer had been talking Wallis had climbed off his stool. He said, "The doctor will object to moving them. Especially the burn case and your Mr. Dickson. It might be better if I explained the reason for moving them in person. . . ."

"Sooner you than me," said Larmer to Wallis's disappearing back.

The ship had picked up more than the usual share of survivors this trip. The poop and upper decks aft, where engineer officers and apprentices, the seamen, and the firemen-greasers all had their quarters, had been forced to accommodate thirty-five R.N. ratings and petty officers together with upwards of fifty survivors from three torpedoed ships. By itself the overcrowding would not have been too bad, but the storm had been such that anyone who was not in a hammock or tied solidly into his bunk was liable to grievous bodily harm—First Officer Dickson being a case in point. As for the bridge deck amidships, the navigation officers, apprentices, and stewards had been crowded out by the additional number of injured survivors who had overflowed from the sick bay.

An added complication had been the fact that the survivors refused to be moved to the more roomy and comfortable tanks below, where the rolling and pitching of the ship was much less violent, and some had refused even to let themselves sleep in case they were torpedoed again. All things considered, Larmer thought they had a point. But the case of Dickson and the two Wren officers was different. They had been in no fit condition to have opinions one way or the other; so the doctor, whose views tended to be medical rather than psychological, had decided for them. But the doctor was a very difficult man to order around, especially when the orders touched adversely on the welfare of his patients. The only thing, in fact, that would make him do as he was told, sometimes, was the few extra grams of gold braid on Wallis's sleeve. . . .

The ship dug her bows into another mountainous wave

8

and the entire forepeak disappeared beneath a solid wall of water which roared along the weather deck, exploding into clouds of spray against the catwalk supports and guardrails until, with most of its energy expended on the deck gear and pipelines, it rolled almost gently around the base of the bridge and tumbled over the side. Watching it Larmer felt a little sorry for the lieutenant commander. As well as having to face an ogre called Radford he would have to negotiate between the bridge and the aft pump room a catwalk, which was the only means of entering the tanks where, amid the tangle of oxyacetylene gear, packing cases, and cargo, the doctor had opened a branch of the ship's hospital. Conditions aft would be somewhat better than those forward, of course, but there was still a strong possibility that Wallis would get his feet wet, that he would get them wet even if he walked all the way on his hands.

There were times, Larmer thought as the foredeck struggled into sight again only to disappear seconds later into another watery mountain, when *Gulf Trader* acted as if she had delusions of being a submarine.

The first torpedo struck a few minutes later just as she was digging her nose in again. If it had waited for another second it would have passed clean over the momentarily submerged fo'c'sle, but instead it hit just below deck about twenty feet back from the prow, and it tore open the deck as if it had been a bomb rather than a torpedo. Several hundred tons of water in the shape of a wave which was then breaking over her bows enlarged the opening, peeling back the deck plating as it if were so much tinfoil and pouring into the underlying forward pump room and storerooms and the big forehold. This time the bows did not rise again and the wave crashed into the bridge with its full force, and at that moment the second torpedo struck the stern.

From the engine-room phone there came a shrill, raucous sound composed of shouts and screams and escaping steam. Larmer broke contact knowing that he could neither give nor obtain help there, and glad suddenly of the tiredness that was deadening his feelings at the moment. The ship, holed fore and aft, was settling rapidly on an even keel. Underfoot the wheelhouse deck was disquietingly stable now, the reason being that *Trader* was going through the waves instead of riding over them. The fo'c'sle was completely under, as were both the fore and aft catwalks, so that the navigating bridge and the boat deck aft seemed to be the superstructures of two different ships. Yet she was in no immediate danger of sinking—tankers were incredibly buoyant. But the sea was running high. She had lost way and was beginning to drift broadside to the waves. That could play hob with lowering the boats. . . .

Larmer unstrapped himself and climbed off his stool, then headed slowly towards the radio room while issuing the only order possible for him under the circumstances. Like his steps, Larmer's voice was slow and deliberate—but not, he told himself wryly, because he was brave or cool-headed or anything like that. It was simply that he was too tired to shout and run about as some of the others were doing. Too tired even to feel really afraid.

Some time later he watched *Gulf Trader* go down, fighting stubbornly every inch of the way. Several times he was sure that she had gone, only to see part of the superstructure heave itself into sight for a few seconds and disappear again. But finally it seemed that even the ship had accepted the fact that she had died and must therefore stay down, and she left the cold and furious ocean to three crowded lifeboats and about twenty rafts.

From one of the rafts, which he shared with the radio officer, Larmer counted heads as best he could and came to the conclusion that nearly everyone had been able to get away. He turned to the other man on the raft then and began instructing him on the necessity of staying alive until they were rescued. The very soonest that they could expect to be picked up was shortly after midnight, he said, and there was no point in surviving a disaster if one did not stay alive afterwards. They had to keep themselves alive, keep exercising their minds as well as their bodies so as to fight loss of consciousness as well as loss of circulation; they had to move their arms and legs, slap each other, tell jokes, sing. . . .

He tried not to think about Dickson and Radford and

10

the lieutenant commander, and the two girls whose names nobody knew.

. . . The main thing, he told the shivering radio officer grimly, was to stay alive until the last possible minute.

II

Seemingly without motion the ship hung like a tiny, metal bubble in a dark and limitless sea, all alone, apparently, and helpless. But the vessel was neither motionless nor alone; it was simply that its velocity relative to the nearest stars was too minute to be easily discernible and the multitude of its companion bubbles were too widely scattered to be seen at all. And within this lonely bubble the years and days were numbered from a historical event and based on a period of rotation which were not that of Earth.

Senior Captain Deslann—senior because he was warm, awake, and theoretically in possession of all his faculties while the other captain was none of these things—looked around the control room and tried to goad his not-quite-thawed-out brain into producing a remark which would sound pleasant, authoritative, and not too stupid. Except for Gerrol the room was empty, the others having left tactfully so as not to embarrass him while he gathered his wits, or having been ordered to do so by the astrogator for the same reason. The wall displays showed nothing in six different directions and Astrogator Gerrol floated respectfully in the center of the control room, also saying nothing.

"If I didn't know better," Deslann said at last, "I'd say we were lost."

A pleasant enough remark, he thought; *but stupid, definitely stupid. . . .*

"*We* aren't lost, sir," said Gerrol, obviously humoring him, "everybody else is. . . ." He hesitated, then went on, "There can be an awful lot of deviation in ten years, sir."

"I expect so," said Deslann a trifle less pleasantly. "How many, and how much? . . ."

Of the fleet of 861 ships launched from around their

home world over a period of three years, Gerrol reported, more than two-thirds of this number appeared to be on course and maintaining proper station—a fact which reflected great credit indeed on the guidance-system technicians. He gave details of the stragglers, their numbers, degree of deviation and estimated present positions. He mentioned the two ships which had suffered catastrophic pile malfunction during the initial period of acceleration and the five others which had deviated so badly that they lacked the fuel reserve necessary to correct, but with these Gerrol did not give details. They both knew how many people each of those ships had contained.

Even in the leading contingent of the fleet, of which they were the most important unit, there was no ship within visual distance of another. The main body of the fleet lay about three years behind them, so that the radioed course corrections required days to arrive at the ship in question and for the acknowledgement to return, and the degree of scatter could get worse.

"In my opinion we should have been stationed at the center of the fleet," Gerrol went on, "instead of in the middle of the first wave with the—uh—expendables. It would have simplified our job, sir, considerably. After all, we are navigating for the whole fleet. . . ."

"*You* are navigating for the fleet," Deslann broke in gently. "You have sole responsibility, so there is no need for you to share any of the credit." He paused as Gerrol wriggled briefly at the compliment, then went on, "As for our position in the formation, the reason might be that you would be expected to take slightly greater pains with your astrogation if you personally are the first to suffer by a mistake. Our psychologists have some funny ideas at times."

"They do indeed, sir," said Gerrol, with feeling.

Such as forbidding all personal contact between the two captains carried by the ships in the fleet which had crews. While Captain Deslann was being warmed Captain Gunt had already been cooled, because the psychologists held that a captain was, and of necessity had to be, the sole authority on his ship. They maintained that discipline and efficiency would be seriously undermined if even for a short period the ship possessed two supreme and equal

13

authorities. Apart from the effect on the crew there was also the possibility that the two supreme authorities might disagree regarding the handling of a problem and ultimately resort to violence as a solution. As well, and to guard against the opposite eventuality, the two captains were forbidden to leave taped messages or even advice for each other because of the danger of their discussing things in too much detail, of sharing responsibility too much until finally the buck was passed back and forth so often that it became lost and the ship with it. Deslann was not even supposed to talk about Gunt to the other officers, and vice versa.

Deslann could appreciate the psychologists' position, but he thought that some kind of transition period should have been allowed—even if only half a day. A short talk with his predecessor would have been of great value to both of them and Deslann did not see how such a brief discussion between equals could end in their biting lumps out of each other's tails.

Psychologists, he decided, had a very low opinion of people.

But if he could not speak to the other captain there was always Gerrol who, as astrogator, was second in command to both captains. Talking things over with Gerrol would be a delicate business, however, since he would have to discuss his predecessor's work with neither of them admitting the other captain's existence. Still, it would have to be done and the time to begin was now.

"The crew?" asked Deslann suddenly. "Are any of them cold yet?"

"Warm, sir, all five of us," Gerrol replied. "We thought it only proper to wait until you . . . until he . . ." The astrogator faltered, aware that he had almost committed the unforgivable sin of mentioning the other captain, then went on quickly, "We've been very busy, sir, you understand. Post-acceleration checks, periodic checking of each refrigeration unit, observation, computation and transmission of course corrections to 800-odd ships—corrections which had to be made many, many times.

"There was a lot to do, sir," he went on, "and the time passed very quickly for us. But now all that can be done

14

has been done, so far as the fleet is concerned. Present deviations are so small that they will require several years to become manifest, so that there is no longer anything for us to do that warrants continued aging on our part. Provided you have no orders to the contrary, sir, we would like to pay our respects and . . ."

"Very sensible," said Deslann, breaking in, "but it will have to wait until after my inspection and you have all submitted your reports. . . . I take it that you all wish to be cooled as soon as possible, that there are no individual projects needing to be tidied up?"

Deslann had to remind himself that his crew had already experienced ten years of shipboard life, while he, so far as his conscious mind was concerned, had only just arrived. He did not believe that he was becoming afraid of being the only warm and conscious being in the whole ship; it was simply that he would have preferred that his approaching solitude come in easy stages. At the same time he could not *order* one or more of his officers to spend precious biological time with him simply because he wanted someone to talk to. . . .

"Nothing of importance, sir," Gerrol replied. "Most of us think the sooner the better."

"Most of you? You mean it isn't unanimous?"

"No, sir. One of the officers objects to being cooled. He says that he has given his reasons to the cap—— . . . I mean the other . . ." Gerrol floundered for a moment, then ended awkwardly, "I'm very sorry, sir. I . . . the details of the incident will no doubt be in the captain's log. . . ."

While concealing his amusement at the other's near panic at mentioning the one-who-must-never-be-mentioned, Deslann was having some mixed feelings at the news. He could not decide whether to be pleased at the possibility of having someone to talk to for a while or angry at his predecessor for handing him what might, by the sound of it, turn out to be a major problem. And, much as he would have liked to have gained a general idea of this problem from the astrogator, he knew that this was impossible at present. Gerrol was far too embarrassed by his slip to discuss anything which might have a close connection with Captain Gunt.

Psychologists!

Aloud, he said, "The private log can wait until after my inspection, a duty which I shall perform forthwith. Follow me, if you please."

The quarters of the crew and himself together with their adjoining cold rooms did not detain them very long, even though Deslann was particularly thorough in his inspection of the refrigeration units and their associated timing devices—there were three separate and supposedly foolproof timers to each unit, just in case one or even two of them proved faulty. Such an occurrence was unlikely, but if the individual members of a ship's crew could not be warmed and revived at an exact and precalculated time, their tremendous fleet might just as well never have set out. The communications room, built into the middle of a computer which filled five entire deck levels, required the longest time of all—even though he was unable, because he lacked the specialized knowledge, to give it more than a cursory check-out.

It was from Communications that the course corrections signals went out to more than eight hundred ships, including the fifty in the advance contingent which did not have crews and therefore had to be controlled remotely. And it was the computer, its two specialist operators, and Gerrol—not necessarily in that order of importance, the way Gerrol told it—who produced the data for these corrections. The engineer helped with computing and communications, since the power room would be fully operational only during an approach and landing, and the ship's medical officer was also helping out—through sheer boredom, Deslann suspected, because the crew were in good health and the passengers were where aches and pains and bacteria could not reach them, far below freezing point.

Before continuing aft Deslann chatted with the other officers, but briefly, because he did not want to acquire any strong impressions of them before he had a chance to study their personality outlines in the private log. Not that he had much chance of talking anyway, since Gerrol was doing most of it! There were several occasions when Des-

16

lann found it hard to conceal his irritation with the astrogator and felt like reminding him that, while it was quite true that this was his first look at this particular ship, he had been very thoroughly briefed and had had intensive training on a ship identical with this one before being cooled. Gerrol kept talking to him as if he were a cadet who had yet to shed his first scales!

In the passenger well, however, Gerrol stopped talking. It was a place for silence.

Because so much space was taken up by the computer, Deslann's ship carried two hundred rather than the customary five hundred passengers. As he dived slowly past the tiers of iceboxes—there were no fancy timers, no sophistication at all on these units—and felt the cold being conducted from them, Deslann began to think some very disquieting thoughts. In a way all these people were dead. They had come willingly, even eagerly, on board ship ten years ago and died. Life had stopped for them then and should some unforeseen catastrophe occur and the crew with their complex, foolproof timers be unable to revive them, they would remain dead. There was no way of their ever knowing when they became permanently instead of temporarily dead.

Or were they truly, physiologically dead in their Cold Sleep? Was it not possible, despite the halting of all life processes, that they dreamed? It might take a whole decade for a single thought or a mind picture to form, and as long again to dissolve, but *something* must be going on in the frigid subconscious of those frozen minds, incredibly slow and faint though it must be—something which furnished a tenuous link between an outwardly dead body and the living soul. . . .

"This officer who objects to being cooled," Deslann said suddenly, "is it, uh, a religious matter, do you think?"

"No, sir," said Gerrol, his tone subdued by their surroundings. "So far as we can gather—he hasn't given *us* his reasons, you understand—he wants to complete a private line of research. It's the medical officer, sir."

Is that all! thought Deslann, and continued with his inspection feeling much relieved.

It looked as if he were going to have company for a

17

while after all, and without having to pull rank to get it. At the same time, if the medical officer proved to be unpleasant company or if his research did not merit the continued use of biological time—time that would be infinitely more precious at the end of the trip than it was now—Deslann would have no hesitation in pulling rank to end it. But there was no sense in trying to decide how long he should allow his medical officer to remain warm when all he had to go on at present was a brief meeting and a few words of conversation. The time to decide things like that was after he had studied all the data available in the private log.

The private log was restricted to the captains of the ship and contained, in addition to the captains' notes regarding their officers and the operation of the ship, a complete and detailed personality outline of each crew member. The psychologists had not hesitated to make recommendations for the various courses of action should anything go mentally amiss with the ships's officers, but where Captain Gunt had added his data there were, of course, no personal comments or advice just the bare facts.

Concerning the ship's medic, whose file Deslann examined first after completing his inspection, the bare facts were more than sufficient. Reading it the captain for the first time began to appreciate the true wisdom of the Board of Psychology's ruling that there be no personal contact between the co-commanders of a ship. Had the situation been different and had there been a chance for him to meet his colleague face to face for a few minutes, Deslann knew that he would have spent all the time available in telling his co-captain exactly what he thought of him.

Captain Gunt had presented him with a problem, and the more he read the worse it grew.

III

When the first torpedo struck *Gulf Trader* Wallis was at the top of the ladder which connected the aft pump room with the floor of Number Twelve tank, gripping the topmost rung with one hand while the other spun the wheel sealing the watertight hatch set in the deck above his head. He was doing this because it was part of his naval training to close watertight doors when a ship was under threat of enemy attack and also because the pump-room floor was level with the weather deck and there was an appreciable quantity of water sloshing around the place. When the injured were being moved to the base of the ladder Wallis did not want them to be soaked by an intermittent waterfall, or the rungs made more slippery than they were at present. Moving the special patients up to the pump room would be a tricky enough job without adding a wet ladder to the difficulties.

The first hit was like a distant, discordant gong, heard clearly but not felt except as a tingling vibration in the metal of the ladder. But when the second torpedo struck the engine room, which was just thirty yards aft of his position, the noise was like a physical blow and the ladder seemed to jump away from him. As he fell backwards his right leg slipped between two of the rungs and instinctively he hooked it over the lower rung, gripping it tightly in the fold behind his knee. The result was that his head described a wide arc which ended sharply on another rung lower down. Wallis was unconscious during the remainder of the fall and did not know that his left arm snagged another rung, which turned him right side up again, and that when he landed at the bottom of the tank twenty feet below it was roughly feet-first and he was so relaxed due to his unconsciousness that he did not break anything.

He came to with a pain in the back of his head and

regular, stinging pains which were much worse, affecting both sides of his face. The features of Lieutenant Radford came gradually into focus as he opened his eyes and a few seconds later he realized that the doctor was slapping his face, hard and rapidly, with both hands. Wallis was so shocked that it was several seconds before he could even speak.

"In-insubordination," he managed finally.

"Resuscitation," said Radford.

Some of the tension seemed to leave the doctor's face and he went on quickly, "You've been out about twenty minutes, sir. We've been torpedoed—one in the stern and I think one up for'ard. After the big bang there were a couple of dull thumps. They sounded like steam explosions, so the engine room must be holed. I'm telling you this in case you're still a bit dazed, you may know about it already. Do you think you can stand up?"

"Yes," said Wallis.

With the help of the surgeon lieutenant on one side and the ladder on the other he managed to stand up. While doing so he kept his eyes tightly shut, wondering if his head was going to split down the middle or just fall off. When surprisingly it did neither, Wallis was able to concentrate again on what the doctor was saying.

". . . No way of knowing the exact attitude of the ship with all this pitching and rolling, but I think we're down by the stern," Radford said hurriedly. "I tried to open the pump-room hatch, but there's too big a weight of water up there for me to push open the seal. We can't get out at this end and I don't know anything about the geography of these blasted tanks beyond the sick bay in Eleven. Is there another way out?"

The picture of what had happened was becoming clear to him, but somehow he did not feel any of the uncontrollable panic that he expected to feel in such circumstances. Perhaps he was just too tired for panic, or not yet fully conscious. Dully, he said, "Amidships. Number Five saddle tank, port side. . . . But no, we can't use that. . . ."

During the storm the cargo had shifted in that tank. The narrow, steep-sided passage which had been dug out of the cargo and which joined the tank entrances at floor level to the ladder from the deck above had disappeared under an avalanche of dried-egg crates and bean sacks when its walls caved in. It would be possible to clear a way to that ladder, but not with just two men working on it, not in time . . .

"Forward of Number One, in the coffer dam," Wallis went on quickly, stumbling away from the ladder and with Radford close behind him. "There's a ladder running up the dam into the forepeak. It's going to be tricky getting those people up it though: we'll have to take them up piggy-back. The dam is less than three feet wide and there are structural members to stop us swaying up the stretchers on ropes, but it's the best place to get out. With that hit in the engine room we must be down by the stern, and the foredeck will be the last to go under. . . ."

Wallis checked himself suddenly. He was talking too much and too fast. Even to himself he was beginning to sound panic-stricken.

They went from Number Twelve, which was a saddle tank on the port side, into Number Eleven, where the doctor had his special sick bay, and through into Nine without stopping to look at the patients. They were in Seven, another center tank, when the lights went out. But Radford produced his pen-light and used this diagnostic tool with its tiny beam to light the way forward to Number Six, where there were a workbench and a rack of emergency lamps.

In the tanks where they did not trip over packing cases, bundles of cable and scattered welding gear, they stumbled against and cursed and climbed over portions of the *Trader's* cargo, because even in the sections where modifications were currently under way there was food stacked in odd corners. The whole point of the U-boat blockade was to starve Britain into submission by cutting off supplies of food and war material; consequently every available cubic foot of cargo space moving eastward across the Atlantic had to be put to use. Not to have done so would have been tantamount to treason, considering the frightful cost in lives and shipping which had to be paid for the vessels successfully running the gauntlet. In *Gulf Trader's* tanks the available cargo space was small in relation to the ship's total capacity because of the modifications, but the storm had tumbled it all over the place. Climbing over and around it was like running one of the commando obstacle courses, with the darkness and a heaving deck underfoot just to complicate things.

We'll never make it, Wallis thought desperately, *we'll never do it in time!*

Wallis did not know how much time they had exactly, only that it was taking them far too long to reach the fore-hold and that it would take a whole lot longer to move Dickson and the two girls there. Since the fall from the ladder his mind had been confused, but now it was beginning to clear and he felt desperately afraid. The ship was sinking and they had to get up on deck—*he* had to get up on deck! Trying to save the injured, or even Radford, was becoming less important somehow. . . .

They left the watertight doors open behind them as they passed through, to save time during later trips and because all the tanks were free of water. This was a very good sign. Wallis reminded himself of how incredibly buoyant tankers were supposed to be, especially when running empty. *Trader* wasn't empty, her cargo tended to be small, dense, and heavy, comprising as it did food and welding gear, but her tanks were intact and there was a lot of air in them. As well, there seemed to be a definite upward tilt in their direction of travel—she was certainly down by the stern. The fact that he had the sensation of constantly moving uphill might have been caused by extreme fatigue or wishful thinking or both, but Wallis did not think so. As they stumbled through the door between Three and One and saw that the forward tank was as dry as all the others, Wallis began to lose some of his fear and to feel ashamed of what he had not yet lost.

The door set in the forward wall of Number One tank was the same in all respects as the other watertight doors they had passed through, an oval five feet high and two wide whose lower edge was eighteen inches above deck level. The height of this edge had been carefully calculated, it was rumored, to remove the maximum amount of skin from the shins of the people using it, and such doors were generally considered to be a curse and an abomination and an unprintable waste of time—until something disastrous occurred. Now Wallis, while the doctor held both lamps, was spinning back the wheel which kept the lips of the door pressed tightly together, and he was cursing only because this one seemed harder to turn than any of the others.

Suddenly he stopped, aware that one side of his face was wet.

There was water all around the edge of the door, not just a dampness or a steady trickle or even a slow spillage over the lower edge—this was the fine, misty spray of water under pressure.

Wallis reversed his pull on the wheel and tightened it until the spray disappeared. For a long moment he leaned his forehead against the cold metal of the door, hearing the oddly loud sound of his own breathing and, now that he was listening instead of tripping noisily over the gear littering the tank bottoms, the metallic creaking and banging and scraping sounds coming from their freshly murdered ship. Then he turned to face the surgeon lieutenant.

"You don't have to tell me," Radford said suddenly in a slow, harsh voice. "If this ship is riding bows up, then all I can say is that the stern is a hell of a distance down! That water was under *pressure*! We're not sinking, dammit, we're *sunk*! And . . . and . . ." There was a long, tearing crash which seemed to go on for minutes and made the tank around them ring like a cracked bell, and when it ended the ship seemed to lurch under them. The doctor went on, "Hear that? We're going down, beginning to break up! The lower we sink, the higher the pressure. Any time now the hull will cave in—you can hear the breaking-up noises already."

Radford had dropped one of the flashlamps, and it lay on its back on the deck, throwing up a narrow wedge of light between them. The bottom lighting gave the doctor's features a terrifying appearance, like something out of a Dracula picture, and it was only afterwards that Wallis realized that this was due to the light and that his own face must have looked just as bad. But at the time he was too frightened by the demoniacal aspect of the lieutenant and

23

of what he might do if, as seemed likely, he went berserk to think of anything beyond the immediate necessity of calming him down.

"I . . . I disagree. Doctor," Wallis said, trying to keep his voice steady. "The watertight door is at the bottom of the coffer dam, and if the dam was flooded with the ship on the surface and completely undamaged there would still be considerable pressure down here. And we are *not* sinking—or if we are it is very slowly! The pitch and roll is as bad as it ever was, and if we were even a short distance below the surface the wave motions would have been damped out. My guess is that we're completely awash, maybe with just the poop and bridge decks showing—these tankers are very hard to sink, you know—and we could drift that way forever."

It sounded good, Wallis thought. So eminently sane and logical that he was beginning to believe it himself. When he went on his voice was steady and quietly confident.

"As for the breaking-up noises," he said, "I think you are mistaken there. Breaking *off*, yes, but not breaking up. The bows have been hit and the torpedo probably blew the whole forepeak off the ship. The noises we hear are loose plating and deck gear being pushed about by the waves. Some of it is breaking off and falling away. And good riddance, because the more we lose the greater will be our buoyancy and the higher we will ride in the water. . . ."

Neither of them spoke for a long time after that. The motion of the deck caused the lamp to slide away and the lighting on the doctor's face became less stark. The mad glitter went out of his eyes and the features softened until they again became those of the dour and competent surgeon lieutenant whom they had all known but had not exactly loved. Finally Radford spoke.

"If you think there is no immediate danger, sir," he said stiffly, "I will return to my patients."

Wallis nodded. He said, "I'll join you later. At the moment I'd like to have another look around. . . ."

But when the doctor and his lamp disappeared into Number Three, Wallis did not do anything for a very long time. Alone at last, he was having a fit of the shakes.

24

IV

Someone had tied the girls very securely to a raft when their ship had been going down. Possibly the same person had tied himself to the raft but had not been able to do such a thorough job of it and had been swept off, or maybe he had not been able to hang on, or had not wanted to hang on, when the raft drifted into the patch of burning oil. But someone had kept his head amid the flames and explosions and roaring steam to spend precious minutes seeing that two girls were given a chance to live. There was very little known about this person other than that he had been a Lascar seaman with a badly scalded face. The dark-haired girl had babbled this information several times during her delirium even though the doctor had failed to elicit from her her own name. The blonde girl had not spoken at all.

"We must speak quietly," Wallis said, looking at the two bandaged figures across the room. "This will have to be broken to them gently or they might . . . Well, they've been through a lot."

Radford nodded silently.

From the stretcher which lay on the deck between them First Officer Dickson, his head bandaged, his left arm splinted, and his cracked ribs bound tightly with tape, said, "I couldn't talk loud . . . if you paid me."

In all probability it was late in the day after they had been torpedoed, although they were not sure of this because the doctor had banged his watch against the coaming of one of the watertight doors and there was now no way of telling the time. But enough time had passed for the early feeling of panic to disappear. Panic, it seemed, was an extremely violent and short-lived emotion. When it was not followed shortly by escape or death or some other form of relief it degenerated quickly into simple fear. And when their surroundings remained steadfastly, monotonously the same—no change in the attitude of the ship, no failures of watertight doors, no threatening occurrence of any kind—even their fear began to subside.

Wallis had spent a long time going through the tanks and searching among the cargo and equipment they contained for he knew not what. And while he was searching Nine he had heard voices coming from the sick bay. He had joined the doctor there to find that Dickson had come to and was demanding to know why the engines had stopped. Together they had talked to him until his panic also became simple fear and the fear, like that of their own, subsided into a sort of intense, gnawing anxiety—the state of mind, Wallis thought, that a person might have if the doctors had given him only a short time to live.

After that they had opened a can of powdered eggs and made tea by boiling up a kettle with a blowlamp. Because they were all very tired and there was no good reason for staying awake they had gone to sleep then, and the fact of their sleeping made them morally certain that this was another day. And now Wallis was faced with the problem of talking about the future in terms of hours and days and weeks when there was no way of measuring these periods of time.

"To begin with," Wallis said quietly, "we must accept the fact that we are in a dangerous but not hopeless position. We are drifting submerged or partly submerged, judging by the wave action we feel—either the sea above us is rough and we are a short distance below it, or it is calm and we are practically on the surface. The important thing is that if we can feel waves a whole day after being torpedoed we can be fairly sure that we are not sinking."

At least, he added silently to himself, *not very quickly. . . .*

Aloud, he went on, ". . . And that the hull is buoyant at a depth which is too small for us to be in any great danger from pressure. All the tanks are dry inside—not a sprung seam or a sweating rivet anywhere. We are in no immediate danger, and anyone who has been adrift

26

in an open boat in this weather might consider us lucky. But there is still the problem of getting off the ship."

Perhaps he sounded too bright and confident, Wallis thought suddenly, and perhaps he was talking this way to reassure himself as much as any of the others. It was likely that the doctor was aware of this self-deception, too, judging by the sardonic twist of his mouth. Dickson was holding one of the lamps in his good hand, directing the beam upwards, so that very little light reached his own face. Wallis could tell nothing from the first officer's expression beyond the fact that his eyes were open.

Wallis continued, "There are three possibilities here. The first is that we devise some means of signaling our predicament to someone on the surface. Second is the possibility of our being towed home. The *Trader* is a very valuable ship and if the anti-submarine patrols report us several times as in a derelict but not sinking condition they might send tugs and an escort vessel to tow us home. The third possibility is that we drift aground on sand or shelving shoreline with our superstructure exposed—"

"Suppose we run aground on rocks," Dickson cut in. "The west coast of Ireland . . . has stretches . . . that could tear the bottom out."

"That is a possibility, too," said Wallis.

"And another," Radford put in softly, "is that we won't run aground at all, and will continue to drift indefinitely. There is the matter of food, water, and air, sir. How long before our air goes stale?"

Wallis had been devoting a good deal of thought to these questions, and he said carefully, "Let's consider the worst that can happen, that we drift submerged without being spotted or running aground for a very long time. First off, food is not and never will be a problem: we have hundreds of tons of the stuff. As for air, well, this is a large ship with a lot of empty space in its tanks. You might liken it to being locked in a cathedral with all the doors and windows sealed, and ask yourselves how long it would be before the air grew stuffy. Then as well as the air in the tanks there are the cylinders of compressed oxygen used with the oxyacetylene gear. I don't know how many there are exactly, we'll have to make an inventory of these and similar useful items as soon as possible, but the forward tanks are littered with them.

"However," Wallis continued more seriously, "while there is no immediate danger from shortage of air, we must take steps to see that it lasts as long as possible. There must be no wastage in the shape of fires for warmth or for heating meals. Instead of direct heating to keep warm we will have to exercise and/or insulate ourselves against the cold. Perhaps you, Doctor, will be able to suggest a high-calorie diet to help us in this when we have a better idea of how the food cargo is made up—"

Dickson raised his good arm suddenly, making Wallis break off. The first officer said, "You're talking as if we had all the time in the world. I don't think we're as water-tight as you think, sir. There is a leak up top somewhere. It's small, but it could get worse, and there may be others like it. The sound of the drip kept me awake. . . ."

Obviously the thought of the leak was bothering Dickson so much that he had practically forgotten about his ribs. He had only stopped for breath twice.

Wallis said, "I know about that drip. It bothered me as well until I tracked it down. There is a section of piping, cut off and sealed at both ends during the modifications, going to the aft pump room. It projects about four feet from the forward wall of this tank at a height of about sixteen feet. The water dripping from it is gritty but not salty, which means that it is caused by condensation . . ."

When Lieutenant Radford had asked for another sick bay to be set up below decks a corner of Number Ten had been partitioned off for him. This had been done by wedging wooden uprights between the metal floor and ceiling of the tank, lacing ropes between the uprights and hanging sacking and old tarps from the ropes so that the new sick bay would have a measure of soundproofing as well as be able to retain most of its heat. Now that the residual heat from the ship's engine room had long since been sucked away by the frigid ocean, the sick bay was the warmest place in the ship. The reason for this was the body heat and respiration of the five people in the compartment, but since the projecting pipe was at the much lower, outer-hull temperature and since the ship was down by the stern, their hot little breaths were condensing on it and dripping off the end.

" . . . which brings us back to our most serious supply problem, that of drinking water," Wallis continued. "That pipe, when we clean off the rust and dirt so as to make the process a little more hygienic, will be an important means of reclaiming lost water. Perhaps the doctor will be able to suggest other methods for reclaiming water when he has had a chance to think about them—"

"I *am* thinking about some of them," Radford broke in, his tone and expression reflecting extreme distaste. "We would have to be very thirsty to use them."

"We probably will be," said Wallis.

There was a long silence after that, during which the quiet background noises from the ship seemed to grow in volume until they became downright obtrusive: the muffled clanking and creaking of loose deck gear and plating, the gurgle of water from the bilges and storage compartments where air was still trapped, and the soft sighing of the slow underwater waves running the length of the ship. It was so quiet that the breathing of the two girls at the other side of the compartment could be plainly heard, while the breathing of the men was visible as well as audible as it hung in the air between them, outlining the tiny beam of the flashlight so sharply that it looked like a miniature searchlight.

Suddenly the doctor spoke. He said, "Distillation is the simplest method, but it has the disadvantage of requiring heat, which means wasting oxygen. However, we know that there were several large drums of water placed down here for the use of the men working on the modifications, because these tanks are not connected to the ship's hot and cold water system, and the men had to have fresh water for cooking and washing when the mess deck up top became overcrowded. We don't know how much there is left, exactly, but whatever is left can be stretched.

"There is a level of salinity at and beyond which water becomes an emetic and undrinkable," Radford went on, "while below this level the salt content does no harm. Since there is plenty of sea water available I propose

29

diluting the drinking water with it so as to . . . What's wrong, Mr. Dickson?"

Dickson was moaning and holding his chest with his good arm. It was a few seconds before he was able to say, "The thought of watering down the water . . . I mean, you oughtn't to make me laugh, it hurts my chest."

"I didn't think it was funny," said the doctor.

"You haven't got broken ribs," said Dickson.

Radford spent a few seconds groping perplexedly for some connecting thread of logic in this peculiar dialogue; then he smiled and said, "Or a sense of humor, either. . . ." They were both grinning at each other now, and one of Wallis's worries began to fade. Morale among the survivors promised to be good.

Dryly, Wallis said, "I think you should take greater care not to make Mr. Dickson laugh, Doctor. Your Hippocratic oath demands no less. However, there *is* a serious side to this business, and the first step is to make a detailed inventory of our resources. This we will begin at once. The doctor and I will work together, both for the sake of increased efficiency and to conserve flashlight batteries.

"You, Mr. Dickson," he went on, "can keep an eye on the patients. I'll find you something so that you can bang on the deck for the doctor if any of them need attention. All right?"

Dickson whispered that it was all right and so a few minutes later they left him with a heavy spanner and a flashlight placed conveniently on his chest to begin the long job of taking stock.

They started in Number One and they intended working aft from there, systematically listing everything they found which might conceivably be of use. But the inadequate lighting and the fact that the storm had jumbled together the contents of many of the tanks tended to slow the work, and several times they came to crates or other containers which could not be examined without moving a lot of overlying stuff. Rather than waste time during the early part of the search on these items they noted their size, shape, and position so that they could ask Dickson about them later.

As *Trader's* first mate Dickson had had access to the

cargo manifest. When questioned, however, he admitted to reading the manifest but said that he could not at the moment remember it in detail, adding that his knock on the head had probably brought on temporary amnesia. The doctor disagreed with this diagnosis, pointing out gravely that the head in question was in good shape physically and that the trouble might stem from one or more forms of congenital idiocy. Radford was going into this subject in detail when Wallis firmly directed the conversation back to the subject of the cargo.

It wasn't that he did not want to give the two men the pleasure of verbally cutting each other to pieces, but the airy persiflage would have to be tamped down to a minimum until some of the more important matters were settled.

It was some time later that the doctor said, "One of the things I don't understand is why they gave us so many electric light bulbs. There must be hundreds of the things. Extra welding gear and tools I can understand, and non-perishable food in the shape of sacks of dried beans, powdered eggs, and tins of Spam. But light bulbs!"

Wallis said, "You must realize that in time of war it's sometimes easier to route large quantities of material to any given destination than small and that, say, two dozen spare bulbs is below the permissible minimum. Another factor is that they practically gave us this ship and carried out the major structural alterations before we joined it at Houston, and generally have been overgenerous with material and assistance. They are friends who have just recently become allies, you see, and it's my idea that a lot of these friends feel they should have become allies much sooner and this is their way of telling us how they feel. . . ."

"That's true," said Dickson seriously, and then he added, "except for the Spam. I think the Spam is their way of telling us that they have not quite forgiven us for the War of 1812. . . ."

The persiflage, Wallis thought, *refused to be tamped down.*

Shortly afterwards they ate a freezingly cold meal, made the patients as comfortable as possible, and prepared to

31

sleep. All the available blankets had been used to keep Dickson and the girls warm, so the doctor and Wallis slept bundled together under a heap of sacking. They lay back to back, knees drawn up tightly against their stomachs, completely covered by the sacking and breathing through two lengths of piping. In this way they were able both to pool their body heat and to warm themselves with their own expelled breath.

But the sacking was coarse and stank of oil, the end of the pipe was shockingly cold even with his handkerchief wrapped around it, and the warm stale air he exhaled gave him a headache as well. When the doctor moved, either because one of the patients needed attention or simply because he was a born wriggler in bed, an icy draught breached the tiny cocoon of warmth which Wallis was trying to build around himself and he would feel like committing murder. And if the doctor did not move he would lie cold and miserable and angry because Radford was asleep and he wasn't.

At such times he would stare into the blackness of his cocoon, thinking about the absolute blackness of the compartment outside it, of the utter darkness of the ship around it, and of the dark ocean beyond that—a sort of triple distilled blackness. It never occurred to him at such times that sunlight might be glinting off the waves a few feet above them. Rocked gently but not lulled to sleep by the wave action on the deck below him he would stare and watch the mind pictures which formed on this perfect, utterly black screen, and he would try to think.

The wave action seemed much less marked than it had been the last time Wallis had tried to sleep. He had a mind picture of the ocean's surface grown strangely calm and he knew that the picture was an unusual one indeed for the North Atlantic in February. A second and more believable picture formed of the great ship, buoyant but in a state of unstable equilibrium, sinking imperceptibly beyond the influence of the waves, drifting slowly deeper as water forced its way into the isolated pockets of air trapped in odd corners of the ship which were not quite so watertight as were the main tanks. He would try to think of some way of dealing with this problem, and if no answer was forthcoming he would shelve it temporarily and think of other problems.

He couldn't sleep and there was nothing better to do.

V

In another ship adrift in an immeasurably vaster ocean there was also a captain who was trying desperately to find an answer. The problems were similar in that they were both in the life-and-death category, different in that in Deslann's case death, if it came, would touch each and every being in the entire Unthan fleet.

Deslann's initial anger towards Captain Gunt had changed to a feeling of angry sympathy, with sympathy predominating. He had come to realize the full extent and implications of their dilemma together with the desperate attempts his co-commander had made at finding a solution. Not that Gunt had so forgotten the rules that he had left a personal message for Deslann, but the private log contained a tremendous quantity of material on the problem since it had first been brought to his predecessor's attention a little over a year ago—all listed in the approved, impersonal manner. These were Gunt's thoughts on the subject. He did not ask Deslann to do anything about it, but at the same time the data made it very clear that Gunt had reached the stage where he had to go cold in favor of the other captain.

The crew, with the exception of the medical officer, had been pressing Gunt for an early cooling now that their work was done, but he could not give permission for this until he told them everything he knew. At the same time he did not want to tell them the worst before the other captain was made aware of the problem—for there was always the chance, the log implied, that Captain Deslann with his completely fresh viewpoint would find a solution which Gunt could not. If a solution could not be found, then Deslann could tell all to the crew and hope that one of them might come up with something.

And if that failed . . .

34

Deslann had been unable to find a solution in six days and, because Gerrol was becoming downright impertinent in his requests to be cooled, Deslann had told all to the crew. Or to be more accurate, he was letting the medical officer tell it while he himself observed reactions and tried desperately not to give up hope.

"But surely there was some indication that this might happen!" Gerrol broke in suddenly. "Hibernation anesthesia was perfected fifteen years ago. The fleet—the whole operation depends on it!"

The astrogator stopped, plainly unable to find the words to describe his feelings of outrage and betrayal. From their positions around the control room the two computer technicians and the engineer were also silent, although not, Deslann thought, because they were slow to grasp the implications. With them it was probably a state of emotional shock. Their personalities were more simple and well-rounded than that of the cold, egotistical, highly intelligent, and of necessity selfish Gerrol, so it was to be expected they would feel this thing more strongly and take longer to recover from the shock of being told that they all were as good as dead.

Looking at each of them in turn the medical officer said defensively, "That is not wholly accurate, Gerrol. The technique was used successfully, but the subject was a volunteer who understood the risks involved. While we were trying to perfect the technique many of the later volunteers were not so lucky as he was. But you must understand that the method had to show only a strong probability of success at that time for the decision to be taken to begin building the fleet. There wasn't enough *time* for the usual lengthy program of testing given to new drugs and techniques—"

"I understand that time was limited, Healer," Gerrol broke in again, "but we were told that the technique was safe—"

" . . . Despite this time limit," the healer went on, looking at Gerrol but otherwise ignoring the interruption, "the technique was perfected and rendered safe *so far as was possible to do so within our own home planet and solar system!* I must stress that point. It is hard to see how

35

the absence of weight could affect a person whose meta-bolic processes have been halted in a Cold Sleep tank—but this might be a factor. It is more likely that subtle differences in background radiation are the cause, or a combination of free fall and radiation, or some factor which we cannot conceive of as yet. Whatever it is it has uncovered a flaw in our suspended animation system. The effects are subtle, but cumulative, and they are serious enough to wreck this whole operation."

"I don't see that," said the communications officer suddenly, speaking for the first time. "The effects are subtle, you say—so subtle that they won't actually kill anyone. Why can't we carry on as planned and hope for the best?"

Bitingly, the healer replied, "There is nothing to stop your going ahead as planned and hoping for the best, for as long as you have enough brain left to hope with—and that won't be for long, believe me! I have now definitely established the fact that with each cooling and subsequent warming there is a deterioration in cell structure, and it is the brain cells which come off worst.

"I have been working on this since the shutdown of acceleration," he went on more quietly, "nearly ten years ago. The tests were conducted with animals, of course, which means that they could not verbally communicate their symptoms to me, but there are methods of physical and psychological probing which render such communication superfluous. The tests covered the smallest lab animals right up to food animals with eight times the physical mass of ourselves. They were exhaustive and left no room for doubt. I was absolutely sure of this flaw even before the captain's warming added final proof."

He looked apologetically at Deslann, possibly because what he was about to say might be a breach of privilege, then went on, "The effect after the first warming is minor. There is a mild, persistent headache which is, of course, susceptible to medication. There is a feeling of mental confusion, also mild, and temporary. It is a little difficult to remember things, but the memories are still available and are complete and accurate.

"After the second warming," he continued grimly, "the

effects would be more—noticeable. Large segments of memory are no longer available and those remaining have faded or become distorted, the most recent memories or training being the first to go. You will all have had experience with aged relatives, and noticed the gradual decaying of mental processes which seems to peel away the more recent layers of memory so that they live increasingly in the past. What is happening here, however—and this is an extreme oversimplification, since none of you are advanced in this specialty—is that the tiny electrochemical charge by which data are stored in the brain cells leaks away, partially at first and then completely, when the brain in question is subjected to repeated hypothermia. After two periods of Long Sleep I would not trust any of you to navigate this ship to the target system, or to land if we got there.

"After the third or fourth warming," he concluded softly, "I wouldn't trust you to get to the other end of the ship. If you were very lucky you might remember how to talk."

And on the voyage it was expected that each member of the crew would be cooled and warmed on an average of twenty times, and anything up to fifty times for the two captains. . . .

Gerrol and the others began asking the questions and putting the suggestions expected of highly intelligent lay people, and Deslann found his attention wandering away from them and from the increasingly testy answers being given by Healer Hellahar. Perhaps it was the effects of his first resuscitation beginning to show, or more likely it was simple autosuggestion brought about by the knowledge of those effects, but his mind seemed bent on dwelling on the period of his late childhood and early maturity.

Not that any of them were old now, because the aging and infirm, the middle-aged, and the unfit had all been left behind on Untha, together with the young people who had elected to stay and those who had not so elected but for whom there were not enough places in the fleet. The people who went with the fleet were very carefully chosen, the people who crewed the ships were chosen with even greater care, and the crew of the flagship was the result

37

of a physical and psychological screening process which had been carried almost to ridiculous lengths. With Deslann the initial testing had started before he had reached maturity, so that he did not have much childhood, and that which he did have had not been exactly happy.

This had been due to the atmosphere of fear and tensions which pervaded his home and his world rather than to any failing on the part of his parents. During the past three hundred years Untha's sun had grown steadily hotter and her two great oceans had shrunk until there was no longer a water connection between them. Plant and animal life had long since disappeared from the land surface and in the sea his people were being forced to occupy an ever narrowing life stratum—between the ocean surface, which was close to boiling point and too hot to allow life without complex refrigeration systems, and the depths where the increased pressure demanded even more complicated forms of protection. And so at an early age Deslann had come to understand the reasons for the atmosphere of tension and fear, and to realize that not only were his people being pressed between an ever deepening layer of boiling heat and the crushing pressures of the ocean depths, they were trying to decide on which of two methods should be adopted to solve the problem. The choice was not easy.

They could bend all of their considerable technology and resources of metal and power to pushing downward, to building great pressureproof cities on the ocean floor, perhaps extending down into the bed of the ocean itself. In this way they could buy a few more centuries of time for all their people before the oceans boiled completely away and the very water they breathed became superheated steam. Or they could throw all those same resources into an attempt to place a small proportion of their people onto another and more hospitable world.

To a people who had had space travel for ten generations the choice, although difficult, was perhaps obvious from the start.

And so a tremendous telescope was built in orbit around Untha, an instrument whose mirror covered a greater area than a large city, and a suitable world had been

38

found. Fifteen generations would come and go during the trip to this planet, but it was cool and its oceans covered four-fifths of its surface and its mass was just right and there were no indications of intelligent life, so that nearer and less-perfect possibilities were not seriously considered. The fleet was built, and during the building the hibernation anesthesia technique was perfected, making it possible to take along many more times the number of people originally intended, so the ships were modified to carry large numbers of passengers who would not require food from the beginning to the end of the tremendous voyage, and great efforts were made to develop foolproof timers for the Long Sleep tanks and remote-control systems for the un-crewed ships.

The plan finally adopted called for full crews only at the beginning and end of the trip, the interim period being covered by individual crew members who timed themselves to wake for a few hours or days every four of five years for the purpose of checking position and correcting the courses of any wanderers. The ship which was to navigate for the fleet had a crew of six, the sub-fleet command ships had three each, and the section leaders had one each, the remainder of the fleet being comprised of un-crewed ships under remote control. In the event of death or disablement or some other emergency occurring in the ships of a sub-fleet commander or section leader there was provision in the flagship for controlling each and every unit in the fleet.

It was to have been the flagship's job to make a detailed study of the target planet during the final approach, to decide on the best landing points and to see that the guidance systems of each of the following ships were set to land them at these points, and then to go down with the leading contingent to establish themselves and carry out the final on-the-spot tests which would aid the settling-in of the later arrivals.

. . . Except that they all might just as well have stayed at home!

Angry suddenly, Deslann silenced the five-sided argument still raging around him by saying sharply, "Since you have only just been made aware of this problem I think it is unlikely you will be able to assist the healer with it just yet. I suggest that you each go to your quarters—you, too, Healer—and think about it. There's plenty of time. Nothing drastic is going to happen until, or unless, you go into Long Sleep. When you have constructive suggestions to make I'll listen to them."

As they swam out of the control room and dispersed, Deslann's mind slipped back again in time to the period when his archeologist father had first taken him on a trip overland to the other ocean. They had used a pressurized and refrigerated land-boat, traveling at night to escape the heat of direct sunlight and sheltering during the day at the bottom of the deep lakes—all that was left of the wide channel which had at one time joined the two oceans. Deslann had marveled at the dry, powdery soil—at home *dry* substances could not be found outside a laboratory— and at the fact that the incredibly thin gaseous mixture which stretched from the land and sea surface out to space had once been capable of supporting plant and animal life, even intelligent life.

But one day they were forced to shelter in a cave instead of at the bottom of a lake and Deslann saw the remains of a family of these strange, gas-breathing land-dwellers. The awkward, strangely jointed skeletons large and small, the containers and utensils of baked clay and bone, and the charred remains of a long wooden structure his father said was a sea boat. His father spoke of the old records which told of these primitive but intelligent beings using such devices to float on the surface of the ocean while their crews speared any of the smaller and more stupid food animals which ventured too close.

This family, his father said, had obviously taken shelter in the cave at a time when its mouth could only be entered at low tide. Here they escaped the savage heat of the day, which had killed the small land animals these people had hunted and made it impossible to grow food, and fished the sea in the cool of the night when low tide allowed them out of their cave. But the surface of the sea would have retained more and more of the heat of the day, and the smaller aquatic animals would have been driven away from the hot tidal areas. There would have been no light in the cave because all the available combustibles had already been burned by the furnace in the sky, and no food, and on days when there was a very low tide the cave would have been filled with near-scalding steam.

They had been intelligent, his father had said, but their level of technology had not been high enough for them to survive.

VI

Approximately eight days after *Gulf Trader* had been torpedoed—Wallis had tried to sleep that number of times and this was the only yardstick he had—the doctor and himself returned from checking the contents of Number Six to find that in their absence the dark-haired girl had come to suddenly and had begun to ask questions. Dickson, who had been lying in the dark so as to conserve his flashlight batteries, had been so startled that he had both dropped the flash and lost the spanner with which he was supposed to signal for the doctor. As a result he had had to answer, as reassuringly as possible, the panicky questions of a girl who was still in pain from her burns and who had just awakened into the frigid, terrifying darkness of a sinking ship.

But Dickson had done very well.

While he was reporting the conversation to the doctor and Wallis it became obvious that he had given the girl a fairly true account of their predicament, but that the truth had been shaded so optimistically as to be almost unrecognizable. Wallis could understand Dickson's reasons for doing this, but it was beginning to look as if the girl had got the impression that their present situation was more ridiculous than dangerous.

Dickson concluded, " . . . and she tells me that she is Second Officer Wellman. As yet I have been unable to discover her first name—I'm a very slow worker, you know, and shy with girls. Would you mind shining your light over here so that she can see how youthful and clean-cut I am?"

Blinking against the light of the doctor's torch, the Wren officer turned her head towards Dickson's stretcher. She said painfully, "Somehow I didn't expect you to be bald."

"That is my bandages, ma'am," said Dickson firmly.

42

"And you're not supposed to make me laugh. Internal injuries, you know."

"Oh, I'm sorry," said the Wren; then, "My first name is Jennifer. Friends call me Jenny."

"Mine is Adrian," said Dickson. "For this reason I prefer to be called 'Hey, you.'"

While the conversation had been going on the doctor moved until his mouth was a few inches from Wallis's ear. In a sarcastic whisper he said, "I've a feeling we're intruding on something or other. Shall we go out and come in again later?"

It was several minutes before the girl spoke directly to the doctor or himself, and Wallis thought he understood why. For a very long time Dickson had been to her merely a disembodied voice in absolute darkness describing the horror of their position in such reassuring terms that somehow she had not become uncontrollably afraid, and now the need to *see* this person was so overwhelming that it far transcended simple curiosity. But eventually she began to talk to Radford and himself and they learned a good deal about her and the other Wren officer.

The blonde girl was called Murray, Margaret Murray. They were in Communications together and had been on a course designed to make the Service language and abbreviations of the R.N. and U.S.N. a little more comprehensible to each other with a view to aiding future combined operations.

That was the only reference she made to the future, and she did not mention the present or past at all. It was natural to suppose that the memory of the first torpedoing and being tied to the raft in the burning-oil-covered sea was too recent and too horrible for her to want to dwell on it, but Wallis got the impression that she was quite satisfied with the present and future as depicted to her by Dickson and that she had no inclination to look for a more detailed, and perhaps less optimistic, picture from anyone else.

That "night" as Wallis settled down to worry himself to sleep it seemed to him that his cold and clammy bed was fractionally more comfortable and their many problems just a little less insoluble. It was difficult to understand why this should be so. Perhaps the fact that Jenny Wellman had begun to register more strongly as a young, good-looking girl than one of the two hitherto unconscious patients had something to do with it. Men tended to feel protective towards girls, especially injured, nicelooking girls, and they also tended to show off a bit—in this instance to display more confidence and optimism than was normal under the circumstances. There was also the feeling of sympathy which made men want to hide the worst from them until the last possible moment. Not to mention the fact that an outward show of confidence very often inspired the real thing.

But unpleasant facts did not disappear simply because someone felt like showing off in front of a girl. Sooner or later these unpleasant facts would bring about their deaths. For the chance of being spotted and rescued was a remote one. An aircraft seeing their long gray shadow in the sea would report it, but as a menace to navigation rather than a ship with survivors still on board. It was even more unlikely that they would drift aground and be left high and dry at low tide. If they touched land at all it was likely to be on the rocky Irish or Scottish west coasts during a winter storm, when they would tear open their bottom. And while it was true that they would never die of starvation—they would die of thirst before they ran out of air—it was almost certain that they would all drown long before any of these other fates overtook them.

It wasn't a time, Wallis thought, to feel even a little optimistic. . . .

After they had all had the usual freezing cold breakfast and the patients were seen to, Wallis went to Jenny Wellman's bed and explained the functions and purpose of the torch and spanner, adding that he was going to take Dickson away from her for a short time. When he saw her expression he told her that they would only be two tanks away and that they needed Dickson's more detailed knowledge of the ship's construction to aid them in a possible method of escape—and if she liked she could keep the flashlamp switched on all the time they were away.

A few minutes later when they were in Number Seven, Wallis said seriously, "Last night before I got to sleep I

44

had an idea, but I couldn't mention it in front of Miss Wellman without—"

"I quite understand," said Dickson, equally serious. "It wasn't suitable for discussion whilst ladies were present. . . ."

"Dickson!" began Radford. He breathed heavily through his nose several times but did not say anything else.

Patiently, Wallis went on, "This is a matter we should try to take seriously. Both of you must realize that we are sinking. Gradually, of course, because the hull is showing no indication as yet of a dangerous increase in pressure even though we have stopped feeling the waves. But it is only a matter of time before we reach the point where water pressure from above will force us deeper whether we remain airtight or not.

"I've heard of it happening to subs which dived too deep," Wallis continued. "They couldn't get up again even though they weren't holed and there was nothing mechanically wrong with them; as a result, they kept on going down until pressure caved in their hulls. At present our situation is that of being trapped inside an outsize submarine which is unpowered and sinking, but slowly. Somehow we must increase our buoyancy before we reach the point of no return."

The doctor was watching Wallis silently. Dickson moved the flashlight slightly but made no comment either.

"Down here we are not in a position to lighten ship by dumping cargo," Wallis resumed, "because we can't open the tanks without flooding them. But if we go back to the submarine analogy and consider how a sub does it— that is, by taking on water as ballast in order to sink and by blowing it out again with compressed air to rise— we might work out something using the storage spaces adjacent to the tanks. Most of them must be filled with water by now, but if some of that water could be forced out again we *should* rise."

"I don't know," said Dickson suddenly. All trace of levity had gone from his voice. He went on, "A sub has high-pressure pumps for that work. Can we build a pump from the odds and ends available here, in time to do us any good? And aren't we short enough of air as it is?"

45

Wallis said, "I wasn't going to use pumps—even if we could make them I'm doubtful myself about the time. And I wasn't going to use air. Maybe this idea isn't feasible, so before I go into it I'd like more details of the ship's construction. You were *Trader's* first mate for three years while up to now I've been concerned only with the modifications to the tanks . . ."

. . . *And if there hadn't been so many modifications,* Wallis added silently to himself, *we would be lying on the bottom now like any other torpedoed ship and none of us would have these problems to face. . . .*

The idea for an anti-submarine tanker had very likely originated with some overworked character who had had a hard day in his small back room and too many cheese-and-onion sandwiches for supper. He had dreamed of a sort of super escort vessel sailing within the body of a convoy instead of bouncing around on the fringe. The hold of this anti-submarine capital ship would be packed with special Asdic gear that could be lowered through the ship's bottom so as to avoid interference from the nearby convoy and escorts. A simple device in the engine rooms of the convoy's own ships would produce a distinctive and easily identifiable engine sound which, if there were any confusion, would eliminate friendly traces from the plot.

The souped-up listening devices would be ultrasensitive and highly directional and the length of *Gulf Trader* would give a base line that would allow them to pinpoint any U-boat closely approaching the convoy before signaling the enemy's position to one of the escorts. If the U-boat were to come too close and there were no escort available to head it off in time, *Gulf Trader* would have mounted new, and as yet untested, Y-guns which could heave a depth charge for a distance of three or four miles. Not even the wildest of optimists expected accuracy over this distance, but it was thought that a U-boat commander faced with someone trying to bracket him with depth charges, especially when there was neither sight nor sound of an escort nearby, would be sufficiently perplexed to dive below periscope depth and perhaps go away altogether. In either event there would be enough time for a conventional escort to make contact and do its work.

Wallis had been relieved of his destroyer command and had been given the new ship with the promise of promotion to full commander when she was commissioned. He had not been asked what he thought of the idea generally, merely told that he was to try it out. He very much doubted that their lordships, or any senior Naval officer for that matter, would have given the idea a second thought if the situation in the North Atlantic had not been truly desperate. As things were, however, they had to try everything or anything once, no matter how crazy it might sound: like trimming a 35,000-ton tanker to sail like a submarine. . . .

Although a small part of his mind had wandered away from the subject for a few seconds, Wallis had continued talking, and now he summarized his requirements.

"The compartments will have to be fairly large," he said, "and placed so that we can check their degree of flooding by tapping on the tank walls—we want to know if our efforts are having any effect, and if not when to try elsewhere. The compartments should be watertight on the top sides so that pressure will force the water downward and out, and the pocket of gas remaining will keep the water from entering again. If the top or upper walls of a compartment are open, then the gas will escape and the water will stay where it is.

"We'll use acetylene instead of air," Wallis continued, "because we already have it under pressure in tanks, making high-pressure pumping unnecessary, and we have no other use for it anyway. The tricky part will be drilling a hole in the tank wall and inserting a hollow, tapering plug with a valve at the wide end. We can manage the plug, but ramming it into place while the hole is emitting a high-pressure stream of water will be hectic. Once that is done, however, we can clamp the acetylene tank to the hollow plug and open both valves until it is empty—"

"This isn't an objection," the doctor broke in quietly, "but have you thought of what would happen if we were found and our rescuers used cutting torches on the walls of a compartment filled with pure acetylene?"

"Boom," said Dickson, grinning again.

Wallis shook his head. "We can always tap out a warning in Morse. I'm much more concerned with our present lack of buoyancy, Mr. Dickson."

The mate was silent for a moment; then he said, "Very well. The fore and aft coffer dams and the bilges, in order of accessibility. The intercostals between the tank floor and the actual hull structure—it's like a single-layer egg box running the length of the ship, with the walls in each division containing a three-foot hole to allow access for cleaning out the bilges and for the purpose of saving weight. The upper edges of these holes are about a foot from the roof of their compartments; so there could be a considerable volume of gas trapped there if necessary. And if you pumped in too much it wouldn't go to waste, it would simply bubble into the next piece of the egg box and be trapped there.

"After the bilges," Dickson went on, "there are the storage spaces and ballast tanks on each side of Numbers One, Four, and Seven. Some of these are likely to be more watertight than others, so I would have to point out their exact position to you. This would mean lugging me over a pile of cargo, and maybe shifting some of it; therefore, the coffer dams and intercostal spaces would be less trouble to begin with."

When he had stopped speaking Wallis took Dickson's flashlamp from him and directed the beam around the walls of the tank. He said, "You've been very helpful, Mr. Dickson, but I'm afraid we'll have to modify your order of priority. The for'ard coffer dam is too badly damaged by the torpedo which hit the forepeak. I don't approve your second idea, for two reasons. One, because the air-filled spaces in the ship are all well below the weather deck, so that we must already be in a dangerously top-heavy condition and an increase of buoyancy at keel level could very easily roll us over. The tanks would remain watertight if this were to happen, but the odd pockets of air trapped about the ship would spill out and our rate of descent would increase. Two, the gas trapped in the intercostals would be constantly forced upwards by water pressure so that there would be the danger of contaminating our air with acetylene. This poison gas would be right under our feet. It is very difficult to spot and seal off a gas leak compared to one of water, and if our aiir was contaminated there is no way of replacing it.

"That is why we'll use the aft coffer dam first," Wallis continued. "The gas will be injected as low as possible, will bubble to the top, and there will always be a water seal to keep the acetylene from getting back to us.

"But in case the dam isn't airtight up top or it doesn't give a sufficient increase of buoyancy," he added, "maybe you could point out a few likely compartments here in Seven. The doctor will mark the places with chalk while I start looking for the hardware we'll need."

He stopped abruptly. The tank around them was reverberating to the sounds of frantic banging, the sounds a heavy spanner might make against a metal deck. And above the noise, growing louder and more piercing with each second that passed, there was the sound of screaming. The doctor snatched the flashlamp from Dickson's hand and hurried aft.

"It isn't Jenny," Dickson said out of the darkness, the anxiety in his voice making it sound like a question rather than a statement. "It must be the other girl. . . ."

VII

Wallis moved carefully towards the starboard wall of the tank until the workbench there stopped him, then groped around the top of it until he found the spare lamp. He spent a longer time finding a place to prop it so that its beam would illuminate a useful area of bench, but after that he did not waste any time at all because he had spent most of the previous night thinking about what he had to do and the material available for doing it.

From the sick bay in Eleven the sounds made by the Murray girl continued to reach them, quieter now and interspersed with the gruffer, reassuring noises made by the doctor and the low voice of Miss Wellman backing him up. Jenny might just as easily have joined the other girl in screaming her head off instead of helping the doctor calm her down, but she hadn't. Wallis thought that he approved of Miss Wellman.

"When you were moving the light around," Dickson said suddenly, "I couldn't help noticing that . . . that . . ." He stopped, then finished helplessly, "What on earth have you been doing to the generator?"

Wallis was silent for the few minutes it took him to check the outer diameter of the acetylene tank nozzle against the business end of the handsome, chrome-plated water faucet which had originally served, with about a dozen just like it, in the temporary washroom in Number Three. Being designed for temporary or emergency use, the other end of the tap tapered gradually so as to accommodate several different diameters of pipe, which was exactly what Wallis needed. But to fit the tap to the acetylene tank he would first have to remove the aesthetically beautiful curve which directed the water downwards.

"Sorry, I was thinking," said Wallis. He put the faucet into the vice, found a hacksaw, and went on, "The doctor

50

and I have been working on an idea for producing light and heat. As you know, this generator is a temporary affair used to light the tanks during the early modifications and until they could be linked to the ship supply. The engine which runs it is working but can't be used because it wastes air and produces carbon monoxide. But we've been experimenting with gearing arrangements which would allow us to operate the generator manually—or to be more accurate, by pedaling it with the feet. That framework built around it is to take the two people operating the generator.

"We think it will need two people to bring it up to the required number of revs," Wallis added, "but once there it will need only one to keep it going."

"And there will be enough power," said Dickson, sounding impressed, "to heat the place as well?"

"Well, no," Wallis said. "The effort required to work the pedals will render its operators comfortably warm, maybe even uncomfortably hot. A stint on the generator would get us nicely warmed up before hitting the hammock, or after taking a bath.

"The doctor is becoming concerned about our standards of hygiene," he added. "We're beginning to smell, you know."

Dickson did not reply at once, but when he did his voice was firm with the firmness of sheer desperation. He said, "A bath, a cold, sea-water *bath!* You can't be serious! The-the drinking water will be gone long before our body odors become, uh, mutually offensive, and by that time the air will be stale anyway! If you ask me, our lives are going to be far too short and uncomfortable as it is without risking premature death from pneumonia!"

The hacksaw blade skidded off the polished curve of the faucet. Wallis sucked briefly on a skinned knuckle, then said, "We've been working on a method for reclaiming water and another—the only one possible, we think—for renewing the air. As soon as you're able to walk we'll introduce you to the head we've rigged in Number Two. The idea there is to keep the, uh, solid and fluid wastes separate. When the generator is working we should be able to boil and distill small quantities of water electrically,

51

using a heater element sealed in a glass tube and immersed in impure water. As I've already said, however, the heating of the living quarters will have to depend largely on our own body temperature and more efficient insulation. . . . What did you say?"

"I was talking about your feet," said Dickson, "and grass. There isn't much growing under them."

"I only wish that there was some green grass in here," said Wallis seriously. "It would save us the trouble of trying to grow beans."

"Beans," said Dickson in a baffled voice. "How, and *why?* I thought we had plenty of food."

"According to the doctor," Wallis replied, "we start by soaking some of our dried beans in water, then sow them in a compost of dust, dirt, packing straw, perhaps wood shavings, and, uh, fertilizer. We'll have to take care that the material we collect for this soil does not contain oil or rust as this would inhibit the growth or maybe kill the plants altogether. And we would not be growing them for food. The area of leafage in bean plants is considerable, according to the doctor, who used to grow roses, and green growing leaves absorb carbon dioxide and produce oxygen. As the process requires light this is another reason for having the generator, possibly the strongest reason of all.

"And that," Wallis ended, smiling, "is how we are going to grow beans, and why."

For a long time the only sound was the steady rasp of the hacksaw biting through metal. The voices coming from the sick bay had stopped or had become too low to be heard, and Dickson seemed to have been rendered speechless. But the condition was only temporary.

"I'm impressed," he said finally. "I had no idea that you were looking so far ahead, or working on so many projects. . . ." He hesitated, and when he went on his tone had reverted to that of the Dickson which they knew of old. " . . . What bothers me is that if they are successful, I'll have to take a bath."

Trying to match the other's tone, Wallis said, "We could be rescued before then, or the ship might sink. Try not to worry too much about it."

The doctor returned shortly afterwards. With the bare minimum of conversation he gave his torch to Dickson and asked for directions for marking the positions of the saddle compartments they hoped to use. Wallis, meanwhile, worked at modifying an initial batch of three faucets, breaking off only when it was necessary to help the doctor carry Dickson to another tank. But when the mate's directions were finally complete and it was time to return him to the sick bay, Radford brought up a subject which he had obviously been avoiding since his return from the other patients.

He said, "I can't keep that girl under sedation indefinitely, not just for the sake of peace and quiet. Her burns are still uncomfortable, but not painful enough to warrant keeping her doped all the time. In any case I don't have unlimited quantities of medication and what little there is left I would like to save for emergencies."

The recent movements of his litter and the unavoidable bumps he had received while the doctor and Wallis were pushing and hauling it over scattered heaps of cargo could not have been pleasant for Dickson considering his injuries—so unpleasant, perhaps, that he might have felt entitled to some of the dope the doctor wanted so suddenly to ration. But even though Wallis could sympathize with these feelings, Dickson's reaction came as a shock.

"What the blazes d'you call this!" he yelled suddenly, in a voice too much like the one which had come earlier from the sick bay. "We're trapped in a sinking ship. We're *deep!* The whole damn hull could cave in on us at any minute! What bigger emergency can you have than that?"

"If we were here long enough," Radford broke in harshly, "I can think of several. . . ."

In the following silence the sound of banging came clearly from the sick bay. There was no screaming, just the banging. Presumably Miss Murray was still asleep and Miss Wellman was awake and worried, and wanted someone to come and tell her what all the shouting was about. Judging by the urgency of the banging she could not have been very far from screaming herself.

Wallis motioned for the doctor to take the other end of

53

the litter. He said, "I think Mr. Dickson has need of some female companionship, doctor. To keep him from becoming morbid."

By the time the gear was ready it had been decided that without power for the drills the only way of piercing the coffer dam bulkhead was to burn a hole in it and risk the wastage of oxygen. They decided on procedure and tried to imagine the things most likely to go wrong and to guard against them. There was no way of measuring the passage of time, but Wallis felt that too much of it had passed while the preparations were going on. The deck was so steady under his feet that they might have been hard aground. But the ship was not aground and the waves above them were moving farther away with each hour that passed—and there was no way of telling how fast they were sinking or how many hours had passed or if there was any hope for them at all.

But finally all possible preparations had been made and precautions taken. The cutting torch and tanks and tapered wooden plugs were in place, also the clamps and tongs and strips of thin lead sheeting needed in case the hole was too big and the faucet inlet pipe had to be packed out to size. There was the short length of steel pipe which, when held in position by the tongs, would focus the flame so that it would go through more quickly as well as hold it to the required diameter, and there were the padded hammers and the gauntlets and the face masks which were necessary because when water meets fire there is inevitably a lot of steam. All at once there was nothing left to do but begin.

The hole itself went through very quickly. There was a sudden explosion of steam and spray, then a solid jet of water struck the cutting torch, knocking it away and bursting against Wallis's chest like a high-pressure hose. He staggered back, blinded, and remembered to switch off the torch before he burned a hole in the doctor.

Wallis blinked the water out of his eyes. The doctor was trying to get the pointed end of the plug into the hole and each time he tried the jet knocked it away again. On about the sixth attempt he managed to hold it steady enough so that he could throw all his weight into pushing it into position. Wallis added his weight to that of the doctor's and the jet became a trickle and soon died away altogether. To make sure, Wallis knocked it in tight with the hammer, then sawed off the surplus wood so that the plug was flush with the metal wall.

Checking the diameter of the plug against that of the faucet pipe they found that they had had beginner's luck, because the tapering pipe would fit the hole snugly without being packed. Carefully, they tapped the plug farther into the hole until it was almost through, then placed the faucet in position. With the doctor holding it steady Wallis gave it a good solid smack with the padded hammer. The plug went through to the other side and the faucet inlet pipe took its place, and it happened so neatly that they didn't even get wet.

A few minutes later acetylene gas was forcing its way through the faucet and bubbling furiously up the inside of the coffer dam, while Radford and Wallis had already begun to repeat the process on the wall of the ballast tank adjoining Seven. With each new installation they became more expert and took much less water aboard, but they did not feel more confident. Finally, when acetylene gas was bubbling into supposedly airtight compartments at five different points throughout the ship, Wallis called a halt.

Their efforts were having no effect.

When the doctor, Dickson, and himself were together in Seven again, Wallis said, "The aft coffer dam has had the contents of four acetylene tanks pumped into it and is now taking number five. The ballast tanks on each side of Seven here have had three each, and the storage spaces beside Four have had one each. Some of these compartments already contained air, and we ascertained, as accurately as possible, the water level in these spaces, by tapping and listening for the hollow sounds which should indicate air rather than water being on the other side of the bulkhead.

"The water level in each case was marked with chalk," Wallis went on, "but the water has not gone down to anything like the expected level, despite the volume of gas

55

which we have been pushing into these spaces. I don't understand it."

He looked hopefully at Dickson.

Defensively, the mate said, "Even if the gas escaped from the compartments I picked for you it would still be trapped in the storage space above them—most of it, anyway. I picked them with that in mind. Are you sure your method of finding the water level is accurate enough?"

Wallis did not reply. At that moment he didn't feel sure of anything.

The doctor said, "Maybe the gas in these pockets is so concentrated that it gives back a sound indistinguishable from that of water. If such is the case this gas under pressure will be much heavier, volume for volume, than air. so that we will not gain very much in buoyancy. Perhaps we have sunk so deeply that water pressure has increased to the extent that it will not allow the gas to expand. Or perhaps the gas is forcing the water out, but at the same rate as the water forced its way in, which was very gradually over the space of many days. If that is the case we may not be able to regain our buoyancy in time—"

"Doctor," said Dickson angrily, "don't be so blasted optimistic!"

It seemed that there were to be no helpful ideas from either of them, and Wallis knew suddenly that it had been a mistake to stop and talk like this, that anything which gave them time to think too deeply about their predicament was a mistake. As the superior officer his display of indecision had not helped things, either.

"We have seven more faucets and a practically unlimited supply of acetylene," he said firmly. "We must keep trying."

Sometime later—the doctor estimated it at between twenty and thirty hours, but Dickson, who had had nothing much to occupy him in his litter except holding torches and occasionally talking to Jenny, insisted that it was more like three days—they had to stop trying through sheer fatigue. Despite recent practice each installation had begun to take more time. Radford fumbled his job with the plugs and staggered around the place as if he were half-drunk, and Wallis, through sheer carelessness, neglected to cover

56

his face with the sacking mask and cowl, the result being a scalded forehead. It wasn't a very serious injury, but the cold made it sting.

Back in the sick bay they found the two girls asleep and Dickson wide awake, his teeth clenched tightly, sweating and staring into the darkness above him. He did not look at them or reply when they spoke. Radford shook two tablets out of a bottle, hesitated, then made it four. He said, "You need to go to sleep, Mr. Dickson."

To Wallis he said, "One good thing about all this is that we've been working so hard that we are going to go to sleep warm for a change."

But Wallis did not go to sleep at once or, at first, completely. They had closed all taps and disconnected all the acetylene tanks before returning to the sick bay, but there was still an awful lot of bubbling and gurgling going on all over the ship. Wallis tried to tell himself that this was a good sign, but then he would contrast the total air space within the tanks with the relatively tiny amount by which they hoped to increase it and he would wonder if it was enough. He would argue then that the tanker had been drifting close to the surface for more than a week and if it was sinking only now, it must be sinking very slowly and that surely a minute increase in over-all buoyancy would tip the balance.

But he did not know for certain, and while his mind argued wearily to itself it began to drift more and more frequently into sleep—a sleep composed of a series of brief, terrifying nightmares in which his fear became reality and where the bubbling and gurgling noises became the sounds of their hull breaking up and a solid mass of water crashed down on them and they tore at the metal walls around them and at each other with their bare hands and screamed and screamed. . . .

Eventually his body's weariness would not let him wake himself from these nightmares and somewhere along the way they changed. Wallis dreamed that he was on the bridge of a destroyer somewhere in the Med, to judge by the weather. It was a very pleasant dream, sheer wish-fulfillment. The sky was blue and cloudless, the sea calm with a slight swell, the sun was hot even through his

57

whites, and a patch of sunburn on his forehead itched slightly just to remind him that this wasn't Heaven. Wallis would have been content to stay in that dream forever, but for some reason it began to change horribly, and fade.

The sky darkened suddenly, in patches, as if it were a jigsaw puzzle and somebody was taking pieces away. It was much too cold, he realized, to be wearing tropical whites. And all at once the rail of the bridge felt like coarse sacking and the salt tang of the wind became a clammy, almost unbreathable poison which stank of sweat. But the dream did not fade completely.

His forehead still itched, and below him the deck moved gently with the action of the waves.

VIII

In the Unthan flagship the problem, after twenty days of constant study and twice-daily discussions, seemed no nearer solution. Now it was the first discussion period of the twenty-first day and the engineer had just asked permission to speak.

"Since two coolings will cause such mental degeneration as to make it impossible for us to operate the ship," the engineer said, "my suggestion is that we do not risk putting ourselves into Long Sleep until the process has been made safe."

It was normal for their problem to be restated many times—too many times—during the course of these discussions, but his idea was so glaringly obvious that it must simply be a preface to a more important suggestion. And there was something about the engineer's manner, a peculiar air of tension which was foreign to him, which made Deslann listen carefully to every word.

" . . . I have been wondering," the engineer went on, "if it is possible to correct the malfunction in the Long Sleep equipment or, alternatively, evolve a form of treatment or medication which would negate the equipment's effect on our minds. I realize that this would necessitate the use of an experimental, uh, subject of our species and that this subject might expect to sustain mental or physical injury or perhaps even death. At the same time the reputation and ability of Healer Hellahar, who is a specialist in this particular field, is such that I feel confident that if any harm befell me it would be necessary to the research and therefore unavoidable."

There was a highly uncomfortable silence when the engineer finished speaking, and Deslann wondered why it was that in this sophisticated and perhaps degenerate age an act of bravery could give rise to as much embarrassment as it did respect.

"Your confidence in me is flattering and perhaps misplaced," the healer said awkwardly when the silence had begun to drag. "We do not have the resources aboard ship to conduct such research, nor have I, in my opinion, the ability."

"In any case," Gerrol said in a tone aimed at further dispelling the general embarrassment, "we could not spare you. Every single member of the crew will be required to guide in the main body of the fleet and to land this ship—"

"Then why not simply cool ourselves now," one of the computer team joined in, "and set the warm-up time so that we waken, say, a year before the calculated arrival date, putting everything on automatic. That way we would—"

"Get hopelessly lost," Gerrol finished for him. He went on, "We have insufficient reaction mass for large-scale maneuvering should we arrive wide of the target system. Our reserves are enough only for periodic and minor course corrections."

Somewhere in the depths of Deslann's mind an idea stirred, stretched, then went back to sleep again. Perhaps the idea would be a useless one, but the captain thought that he should drag it out into the light and look at it just to make sure. Meanwhile the conversation was rolling on, drifting inexorably away from the subject which had almost given him an idea. He had to get them back onto the subject, but he didn't know which subject it was.

"Let's go back a little, Gerrol," Deslann said quickly. "You said that everyone would be needed to land the ship and guide in the fleet. But that is not strictly true. You could do without one of the captains."

Abruptly, he stopped. The answer was staring him in the face.

And from the other side of the control room Hellahar said softly, "You could do without the healer, too, Gerrol. The captain might need a little help."

Deslann knew then that Hellahar had seen the answer also, that the exchange between Gerrol and the engineer had given him the same idea and started his mind on the same train of thought as that followed by the captain. They stared intently at each other while Gerrol registered disapproval at his mentioning the other captain, and the rest of the crew talked and pretended the lapse had never occurred. Deslann had often felt impatience with the weird ideas and activities of the Board of Psychology, but one of their members would have been very useful to him just now.

And in the years to come.

When he had dismissed the crew with the exception of Hellahar, Deslann decided to test the healer's thinking. The truth was that his pride was a little hurt because Hellahar had found the answer as quickly as he himself had seen it, and while he realized this was sheer pettiness he couldn't help himself. And besides, the test might show that the healer had arrived at an entirely different, and perhaps easier, solution to their problem.

Deslann said, "Since this is the flagship the crew is the best available. Veritable geniuses of astrogators, engineers, computers, and communicators. Not to mention healers and captains, of course. But they, and we, are going to have to organize this highly specialized knowledge and break it down into easily digestible pieces. It will be a long time before we are able to cool them."

"That aspect does not worry me," Hellahar replied. "They will realize the importance of what they have to do. The thing which concerns me is what *we* will do after they have been finally cooled. Do we pick for physical fitness, or heredity, or a combination of the two?"

As he talked on there could be no doubt in Deslann's mind that Hellahar had arrived independently at the same answer. Briefly, it called for the existing crew with the exception of Hellahar and himself taking the Long Sleep once only, which would mean that the mental effects would be negligible, and being warmed shortly before the target system was reached. Before the cooling, however, they would have to prepare a written and taped record of their training, duties, and knowledge, this data to be broken down and simplified so that the basics would be within the mental grasp of a child.

61

The children and the children's children, who in the generations to come would stand watch in the flagship and keep the great fleet together and on course, would be the responsibility of Hellahar, the captain, and two unfortunate females whose identities were as yet unknown.

Even though the identities of the two were not known, Hellahar was already outlining their personalities by the simple process of eliminating traits which in his opinion were dangerous or otherwise undesirable. Not only had Hellahar got the idea, he was—perhaps because of his specialty—way ahead of the captain in some respects.

Simply picking them at random was out for several reasons, Hellahar said. The choice might be physically or mentally unsuitable. Or if capable of withstanding the considerable shock of being told of the situation and her position in it, the female in question might already be mated and emotionally tied to another Long Sleeper and this would be a psychological barrier too difficult to overcome. Even as it was, warming two females and requesting that they mate with them because the safety of the fleet and the continuance of the race demanded it was not going to be easy. It was very rare to find a female whose thought processes were not colored and to some extent guided by emotional considerations, and they would be unlikely to find two of them who would be willing to accept logical argument as a form of courtship. . . .

" . . . Fortunately for us," the healer went on, "there is a medical profile of each Long Sleeper attached to their tanks, and a great deal of psychological data can be gathered from a purely medical case history—especially when the history gives endocrinological details and an outline of heredity factors. These data give, however, only a general idea of the personalities concerned, which is going to make our final choice a very uncertain business."

As he had been speaking Hellahar's initial excitement had dwindled until now he sounded deadly serious, even afraid.

"First," he continued grimly, "they will have to be in good physical condition. There must be no history of hereditary diseases. They must be psychologically stable, intelligent, and adaptable. At the same time there must be the widest possible difference in their generic background, because from the third generation on there will be the problem of inbreeding to consider—"

"Where," Deslann broke in quietly, "does er, uh, beauty place on this list of yours, Healer?"

Hellahar stammered, fell silent, and gave the captain a long, searching look. Then he said, "With intelligence and stability and good health on the list, the other goes without saying. A physically efficient person is normally, uh, well-constructed—it's a simple matter of good design. And it could be argued that a beautiful female is much more likely to be psychologically stable than an ugly one, so that we are forced to choose the former type.

"Also," he went on, "since females are more susceptible to emotional rather than logical arguments, and since for the best results the emotion in question must be a two-way affair, in my opinion it is vital that we choose the sort of person we can feel emotional about.

"There are many reasons," Hellahar concluded seriously, "why we should pick the best-looking ones."

"I'm glad," said Deslann, just as seriously.

They both laughed then, loudly and long and at the same time a little self-consciously because they both knew there was nothing at all to laugh at in the situation. They were two children laughing in the dark to show they weren't afraid of the Big Black Gobbler. It was a most uncomfortable, unsatisfying laugh, and it was the last they were going to have for a very long time.

For there was nothing in the least amusing about Deslann's explanation of his idea to the rest of the crew, or the more detailed planning and subsequent orders which followed it. There was nothing funny about the responsibility he bore—a little matter of the continued survival or the extinction of his whole race—or about the many second thoughts he had.

"Why can't we simply warm two couples?" he said to Hellahar some weeks later during one of his periods of self-doubt. "That would relieve us of the initial problem with the females."

"Wouldn't work," replied the healer, respectfully but definitely. "We must teach the children, subject them to

63

training and disciplines which will be harsh at times. We could not do that without interference if the children were not our own. Besides, there is still a lot to do before the problem of how best to woo our future mates comes up. . . . "

Which was very true, because they had decided some days previously that the preparatory work of the crew should be completed and the officers themselves placed safely in Long Sleep before the chosen females were warmed —that way it would be less unsettling all round. So in addition to Deslann's efforts to make his officers understand the necessity for leaving behind them a simple yet complete training program for the future generations of astrogators, engineers, computer and communications technicians, Hellahar and himself had the future generations of captains and healers to think about.

Despite this pressure from more immediate problems, Deslann still found time now and again to worry about those females, even though he no longer mentioned his concern to Hellahar. Part of the reason for this was because Hellahar had stopped mentioning the subject to the captain. But it became very obvious one day that the healer was giving this problem considerable thought.

Deslann found him in the recreation room studying a tape, the title of which startled the captain because it was not a work which he had expected to find in his ship, or to find the healer reading. It was *The Life of Targa Wunt.*

"It's rather boring, really," Hellahar said defensively as he saw Deslann's expression. "Just a list of names and dates and repetitious incidents—sheer statistics! But there are passages here and there which could be, well, helpful."

"I'll borrow it when you're through," said Deslann, and left him to get on with his studies.

Targa Wunt had been possibly the worst blackguard and undeniably the greatest lover in all of Unthan history.

IX

Gulf Trader drifted submerged but close to the surface for what seemed like three or four weeks, and during that time there were many changes inside the ship. The lighting was the most dramatic and important change, although the sense of drama was rather spoiled in the early days by the number of failures. But for a few minutes each day to begin with, and then as the various snags were eliminated for as long as there was someone on the pedals, the cold metal walls and littered floors of certain tanks were, to eyes accustomed so long to darkness, brilliantly lit.

Another change was that the patients had become mobile, although in Dickson's case it was with the aid of crutches. The altered privacy requirements together with the fact that they were still down by the stern, and the air in that section of the ship was beginning to go stale, made it necessary to shift the living quarters forward to Number Three, which was partitioned off and insulated with sacking. Everyone said that it was a warmer, more comfortable place to sleep in, although this may have been because the two girls were now able to bundle together for warmth instead of lying on separate litters each "night," and because Dickson was now adding his body heat to the pool under the men's heap of sacking. Another reason for the slight increase in warmth was the double one of the approach of spring and a possible southward drift past the west coast of Ireland.

They had not heard any ships passing since they had been torpedoed—the Atlantic being a very large ocean—but if the drift continued they would arrive eventually in the busy area of the southwest approaches to the English Channel. That was why Wallis had them spending so much time on signaling devices.

When the ship again began to slide dangerously far

65

below the surface the necessary measures were taken almost as a routine drill. The major problems were those of drinking water and air supply, and they worried about those constantly.

And today, thought Wallis irritably, *the subject is going to spoil our lunch. . . .*

Dickson had just said, "How does your garden grow, Doctor?"

It was a question which Dickson had asked, in exactly the same form, far too often for it to be funny anymore—except possibly to Jenny Wellman, who approved of practically everything Dickson said. Wallis took a firm grip on his temper and tried hard to make allowances.

They were seated around the workbench, which had been smartened up by the girls for use as a dining table. A flashlamp hung above it since there was nobody on the generator, and the faces were in shadow while the meal was being spotlighted. They were having a cold stew that was composed of powdered eggs and sea water and that varied, according to individual taste, from the consistency of a thin paste to that of thick porridge, with a cup of tomato soup, also chilled, to wash it down. They had been very lucky in finding the two large crates full of tomato soup cans, because the doctor had insisted that he needed a lot of pure, or at least unsalted, water for his beans. Even so, the meal was like all the other meals, a freezingly cold, unappetizing mess; and having to eat it must have been much worse for Dickson than for any of the others.

They had had a short spell on the generator to warm themselves up in preparation for their refrigerated lunch, but Dickson was still not fit enough to work the pedals and so felt colder and more miserable during meals than at any other time, which was saying a lot. Definitely, Wallis thought, allowances should be made, and from the mildness of Radford's reply it seemed that the doctor agreed with him.

"Not very well, I'm afraid," he said. "All but three of the beans planted in the first tray have taken, although they don't seem to be exactly flourishing. I'm not an expert on plant biology. All I know is that bean plants, when mature, have a large quantity of leaves and these should be good at absorbing our CO_2. . . ."

Radford had not known much about gardening, but he had done everything possible to make those seeds grow. For days he had carried tied to his waist next to his skin the bottle of water in which the dried beans were soaking, and later he had transferred them into tobacco tins packed with his specially prepared soil and carried them in the same place so that his body heat would aid the process of germination. But now his precious beans had been cast out into a cold, cold world.

" . . . At the moment they have light for about one third of the 'day,' " Radford went on, "although it is broken up into hour- or half-hour-long pieces instead of being continuous. This may have a bad effect on them, so we must arrange the shifts on the generator to give them constant light for as long as possible. There is also the low temperature. So far as I know the plants are not injured by a periodic drop in temperature, for during spring and autumn it can become very cold at night, but so long as it remains above the freezing point there is no damage. This constant low temperature, however, must be having some effect. Then there is the quality of the lighting—"

The doctor broke off, looked around the table, and ended on a note of forced optimism, "I'm hoping that the bad effects of the cold and lighting will be negated by the quality of our, uh, fertilizer."

In the dim light around the table it was difficult to read expressions. There was too much hair on the faces of the men, one-half of the Murray girl's face was hidden by the bandages she had started wearing again when the generator began working, and Jenny Wellman was sipping cold tomato soup. It was she who finally broke the silence.

"If your garden doesn't grow, sir," she said quietly, "how long before the rest of the air goes stale?"

"It's hard to say," the doctor replied. "You see, the air astern isn't really foul; to the contrary, it's quite breathable right now, so our reasons for staying away from it may be purely psychological. Of course, we have no lighting there as yet, but, too, the old sick bay has unpleasant

67

associations for most of us while the present quarters are relatively more comfortable.

"Another point," he continued, "is that when the air finally does become foul it will be a very gradual process, due to the tremendous volume of these tanks. The onset of symptoms will also be so gradual that there will be times when our emotional state will exaggerate them to a dangerous extent, and we'll have to guard against this. There is also the possibility that the change will be so gradual our lungs will be able to adapt to it to a certain extent and so increase slightly the time left us.

"All this makes it difficult to give an accurate answer," Radford concluded, "but I would say that we have until the middle of June or early July."

"Thank you, sir," said Jenny Wellman.

Something about the girl's tone, and the expression on the visible half of the other girl's face made Wallis add quickly, "Of course, this presupposes that the garden is a total failure. Even if it were only partly successful in renewing our oxygen, that time could be extended, perhaps even doubled."

"Oh, certainly," said the doctor, catching the ball neatly. "Mid-June is the most pessimistic estimate."

Shortly after that they went to bed, it now being the accepted thing to retire after the main meal, when the psychological reassurance of a full stomach, the calorie content of the food, and the recent exercise on the generator all conspired to increase their physical comfort. It was while the doctor, Dickson, and himself were burrowing into their sacking that the mate asked the question which Wallis himself had been about to ask.

"Doctor," he said, "how do we know when it is mid-June, or July, or even Christmas? Have you found a clock somewhere, or maybe a bootleg calendar?"

Radford paused a moment before replying, then said softly, "Something like that. I'm a doctor, you see, and the girls are my patients—and there's no privacy in this place anyway. Let's just say that we have two fairly reliable biological clocks on board. They are no good on hours or minutes, but they can be depended upon to record the passage of the months.

68

"Now I would like to go to sleep while I'm still warm, if you don't mind."

Slightly more than a month passed and in that time Dickson was pronounced fit to man the generator, the ship began to sink again twice, and a vessel passed over them so closely that if it had not been a shallow-draft mine sweeper or an escort, judging by the sound of its engine, it would have run aground on their navigating bridge. Dickson's spirits improved, although he had a bad habit of asking the doctor "What time is it?" as well as "How does your garden grow?" The decrease in buoyancy was dealt with almost as a matter of course and their near collision gave them a chance to try out their signaling devices for the few minutes it took the ship to pass.

Then one day they found themselves drifting onto the flank of a passing convoy.

They were pretty sure that it was daylight because of the number and quality of the explosions. The convoy was under heavy air attack—the sound of a bomb hitting the deck of a ship having a much softer quality than the sudden, savage shock of a torpedo hit under water. There seemed to be a couple of U-boats sniping at the convoy from the wings as well, and the ocean all around them was filled with the thuds and thumps and crashes of bombs, depth charges, and torpedoes against a background of ships' engines which sounded like the rumble of distant trains.

When the rumble began to die away Dickson was taking his turn on the generator, Jenny Wellman was using a small part of its output for signaling purposes, the Murray girl was also signaling—with a hammer against the inside of the hull—and the doctor was tending his garden. Wallis, who had just come off the generator, was with the doctor. They were all aware that their various ideas for signaling with electrical discharges were unlikely to be effective without an antenna floating on the surface, that the sound of any given ship's own engines would almost certainly drown out the sound of their hammering, and that the ships' crews were too busily engaged to listen to odd noises from under the sea. Wallis had told everyone, including himself, that they should not feel too disappointed if the signals did not attract attention. Wallis did not know how the others felt, but he was so disappointed that he wanted to break something.

Suddenly Radford said, "Mr. Dickson and Miss Wellman have been pestering me, Commander, singly and in small groups, but it's you they really want to talk to. You must have seen what is going on, sir. I think your duty is plain in the matter, sir."

The sounds of the convoy had died away until they were lost in the metallic echoes of Miss Murray's hammering. Three widely spaced blows, three close together, then three spaced out again.

S O S

Wallis said, "Eh?"

"Marry them," said the doctor.

Wallis found suddenly that he had completely forgotten the convoy as his mind grappled with this newer situation, even though it was a matter on which he had already spent a good deal of time and mental energy. But the doctor, apparently, had mistaken his silence for sheer astonishment.

"I realize that the Royal Navy doesn't instruct its officers on how to marry people," the doctor commented, "but I was married and I can remember the important parts of the service. Besides, it's becoming downright embarrassing to watch those two mooning at each other. As things are it's too blasted cold to do anything but hold hands! Supposing that they could find a private spot, and even if they were married and bundled together legally, I still think it's too cold for—"

"I don't," said Wallis sharply. After a pause he retorted, "I had no idea that you were such a romantic soul, Doctor, or that your feelings would blind you to the realities of this situation! When two people marry there are not infrequently a number of by-products. Do you consider this a proper place to bring up children? And how about dealing with a confinement without proper equipment, in this . . . this icebox! And suppose someone dies. Is there any possible way of disposing of the body?"

70

He stopped suddenly as a new thought occurred to him, then went on, "As a doctor you must have considered these problems, and very likely a lot more besides. I'd have thought that you would have been completely against any pairing off down here, utterly against it! The fact that you aren't suggests to me that you have good reason to think that we will not have enough time left to us for these problems to occur, that our Romeo and Juliet should have what fun they can while they can. Do you have reason for thinking like that, Doctor?"

Radford was silent for a long time. When he finally did reply it was not to answer Wallis's question.

He said, "When the Dicksons bundle up it will leave the Murray girl out in the cold, or at least without some-one to keep her warm. Which is a pity, because she is still in a bad way mentally from the effects of the torpedoing. I'd even go so far as to say that her nightmares and general fidgets during the sleeping periods are partly the cause of Jenny Wellman's looking for a new sleeping partner. Only partly, of course. But the fact remains that without the comfort and reassurance of Miss Wellman, the Murray girl's sleep is likely to be seriously disturbed, which means that ours will be likewise. So I was thinking—"

"You can *stop* thinking!" Wallis burst out, with feelings close to panic. "Dammit all, Doctor, are you trying to organize an orgy or something!"

The surgeon lieutenant did not answer that question either. Instead he said, "No matter how long we are here, sir, I don't think that we would ever reach the stage of fighting each other to the death for the only available woman, or anything equally melodramatic. At the same time I can see certain difficulties arising if the matter isn't settled fairly soon.

"You are the logical one, sir," the doctor went on. "Compared with myself, the age difference is much smaller, and I'm married already in any case. You should think about it, sir."

Wallis glared at the doctor and thought about it, and then with equal desperation tried not to think about it. There was no room for thoughts of the convoy or

71

anything else in his mind, even though the sound of Miss Murray's still trying to speak to it filled the whole ship.

Bang-bang-bang, she was saying doggedly: Bang, bang, bang. Bang-bang-bang. . . .

X

Surgeon Lieutenant Radford could not make everyone agree to taking a bath, but he won a minor victory by getting them to periodically change their clothcs. It was a matter of added warmth, he had insisted, as well as of simple hygiene. The uniforms which they stood up in—and lay down in and did everything else in—were so dirty and greasy that they were poor insulators at best, and in their present surroundings the heavy serge would be impossible to clean. Besides, it was a well-known fact that a light, open-weave garment was warmer than a thick, closely woven type provided that there was protection against moving currents of air. He did not have to remind them that *Gulf Trader* was singularly free from moving currents of air.

The new outfits were made from sacking and took the shape of a one-piece coverall with an attached hood. They were washed in sea water and dried by first battering them against the nearest bulkhead to remove most of the water and then whirling them around rapidly in the air. As well as keeping the people warm who were not serving on the generator, the doctor said that the constant washing and battering dry would soften the fibers of the sacking so that they would soon feel comfortable against the skin.

But they found that each needed two of these outfits worn one on top of the other to keep warm, and the girls were kept busy making them for a long time. Dickson began talking about sweatshops and poor, down-trodden workers and his plans for forming a union for their protection, several times a day. Marriage had not changed Dickson's sense of humor, Wallis thought: it was still lousy.

Apart from working the generator and sewing sacks

73

together there was not very much for them to do except think about their troubles; and that was something to be avoided, because they had so many that to dwell on them was simply asking for more trouble—such as the Murray girl's crying in her sleep, their sitting and either staring silently at nothing or arguing endlessly and senselessly about nothing at all until they were close to murder.

The time, according to the doctor, was late May. It was a little warmer in the ship, but still bitterly cold. The air was definitely going stale.

Wallis lay with the doctor under their heap of sacking and tried not to think about these things. What little experience he had of air going foul told him that it should be hot and stuffy and that he should have a dull headache and be inclined toward shortness of breath. He was sure that his breathing was faster and there was no doubt about his headache, but the air was so cold that it did not seem to be stuffy at all. In these circumstances it was hard to tell just how foul the air had become or to estimate the time left to them before it became unbreathable. At the same time there was always the possibility that it was not nearly so foul as he thought it was, and that it was bad mainly because he thought about it too much.

But it was difficult not to think about things. All around him there was silence and he had to listen hard to hear the sighing and gurgling sounds of the sea pressing against their hull, the even breathing of the doctor beside him, or the low muttering that told of Miss Murray's having bad dreams again. Wallis was beginning to feel comfortably drowsy. He thought that if he could find something pleasant, or at least constructive, to think about he might go to sleep.

In some ways their position was similar to that of survivors in an open boat. In a lifeboat there is food and water enough to live, but men grow cold and sleepy and die if they don't find ways of exercising their muscles and keeping awake. In *Gulf Trader* it was their minds rather than their bodies which needed the exercise if they were to continue to survive, and, just as in the hypothetical lifeboat, the exercises they performed could be utterly senseless in themselves.

74

He fell asleep thinking about guessing games and ideas more suited to a children's party than to the dark and frigid hold of a sunken ship. . . .

Wallis was awakened he did not know how much later by the sound of Miss Murray's crying. It was not a loud noise, just the low, gasping, sobbing sound of someone who is trying vainly not to make any sound at all. Miss Murray didn't like disturbing people, and usually everyone kept still and pretended to be asleep so that she would not feel bad when she did. But tonight she was crying so quietly that everyone but Wallis seemed still to be asleep, so he didn't even have the comfort of knowing that he was not suffering alone. The sound went on and on, stopping only long enough to let him hope that she had gone back to sleep, then starting again.

After what seemed like hours of listening to her and staying perfectly still Wallis could stand it no longer. He wriggled carefully from under the sacking so as not to let the cold in on the doctor and sat up in the darkness.

He had no idea what he was going to do or say to her that would make her stop crying, only that he had somehow to put an end to that terrible, not quite silent sobbing before it made him run amuck. A few quiet words of reassurance might do it, or a pat on the back, or a gentle reminder that she needed her sleep, that they all needed sleep. Then again, that might simply make her worse. The thought came suddenly to him that if he did anything at all, considering the highly nervous state she was in, she might get the wrong idea and start screaming that she was being assaulted or something. But when he found the torch and switched it on he saw that she was sitting up, wide awake, and shivering. Her arms were folded tightly against her chest, her head was bowed so that her cowl hid her features, and the only motion about her was the constant steaming of her breath.

Wallis moved across and gently shook her shoulder. He had to do it several times before she took notice; then she said, "I'm cold."

A number of angry and impatient replies rushed to Wallis's lips, like weren't they *all* cold and what did she

75

expect when she was sitting on top of all the blankets instead of lying inside them? She had been given all the sick-bay blankets to make up for the loss of Jenny, and they were much warmer than the sacking everyone else had to be satisfied with. But Wallis fought back the things he wanted to say and said instead, "I've been meaning to check the water level in the coffer dam. Maybe a walk aft would warm us both up. . . ."

As they were passing through the old sick bay into Number Twelve and they both began fighting for breath, Wallis said, "The air is quite fresh. If we die of asphyxiation it will be purely psychological."

She gave a small laugh, the sort a junior officer has to give when a senior makes a crack which is supposed to be a joke.

After they had checked the coffer dam bulkheads and climbed up and down the ladder often enough to be fairly warm, Wallis stopped her as they were returning through the sick bay. He pointed to the litter which had belonged to Dickson and asked her to sit down, then hooked the torch onto a projecting pipe and sat beside her. Not too close.

After a couple of false starts, he said, "You know, being caught down here when the ship was torpedoed was probably a good thing for us. If we'd been up top the chances are that we would have spent some time in the water and a much longer time, maybe three or four days, in a lifeboat or raft. We might not have survived that, and you girls certainly would not have done so, injured and unable to exercise as you were. You're still alive and you could have been dead.

"I know it's cold," he went on, "and the air is going foul. But summer is coming and the doctor is beginning to show results with his beans, and we have plenty of food and just enough water and we're dry. It might be a long time before we're rescued, but we will be, eventually. So there is nothing immediate to be afraid of, nothing for you to lose any sleep over. . . ."

There was no response for a long time; then she said, "I understand, sir. We can't get torpedoed again down here."

Wallis grinned suddenly. "That's it exactly," he said.

"I used to be good looking, you know," she said. "And I know what a burned face looks like. My . . . my boyfriend bailed out of a burning plane. His face was . . . was . . . He used to tell my parents that we were Beauty and the Beast."

His smile must have looked somewhat strained, Wallis thought, as he said, "It says a lot that his looks didn't matter to you. Even so there are going to be a great many people scarred by this war, and war-scarred heroes earn special respect. The same applies to war-scarred heroines, although in their case the plastic surgeons would make an extra effort to repair the damage. But you're lucky. If the surgeons can't fix you up completely, and the doctor tells me that they probably can, you'll be able to compare operations with your boyfriend."

His tone must have been a bit too hale and hearty, too insensitive. She began to cry again. Wallis put his arm across her back and patted her shoulder awkwardly. The movement caused her cowl to fall away from her face, revealing the devastated left side spotlighted by the hanging torch. Even the hair on that side was affected; it was gray at the roots and patches were missing, and the only good thing about it was that it hid her damaged ear. Wallis had helped the doctor to dress that ear a few times and he didn't particularly want to look at it again. But the most horrifying thing about the Murray girl's face was that the right half of it was smooth and unblemished and beautiful.

"I'm sorry," said Wallis. "I shouldn't joke about things like that."

"We were engaged," she said suddenly. "Just before he was killed."

"I'm sorry," said Wallis again, wishing that he was dead himself, or somewhere out of this acutely embarrassing position.

"Don't be," said the girl. "I didn't like him very much. But he felt so awful about his face that it seemed the right thing to do at the time. I used to tell him that his bad looks made my good looks better by comparison, and it

77

made him laugh sometimes. But the second time he was shot down he wasn't able to bail out.

"Maybe he would have wanted me—he knew what it felt like to be this way," she went on, so quietly that Wallis had to bend closer to hear her. "But nobody else will. Your war-scarred heroes will want, will deserve, Beauties, not another female Beast like themselves. I can't see myself, but the side of my mouth feels tight and my eye feels wrong and my face is . . . is like the bark of a tree. Can you imagine anyone looking at it without wanting to turn away and be sick? Can you imagine anyone wanting to *kiss* it?"

"Yes," said Wallis.

The trouble with a lie, he thought, is that if it is to sound like the truth it has to be supported from several different directions. Well-meaning, kindly lies seemed worst of all in this respect. All he wanted to do was to make her feel better, from motives selfish as well as selfless; he wanted to stop her crying so much and upsetting everyone, and to feel better generally, and to stop having the bad dreams which kept her and everyone else awake. Merely telling a lie, though, he knew instinctively, would not be enough. Radford and Dickson would never know how hard he was working to ensure their sleep.

Briefly, lightly, he kissed her on the mouth.

She did not seem angry, or surprised, or anything in particular. Wallis felt that his lie was not convincing, that he was making a proper hash of things generally. He said brightly, "You kept your eyes open. I thought all girls closed their eyes when they were being—"

"I wanted to see if you closed yours," she said dully, "and I think you did. You couldn't look at me close up and you couldn't bear to touch me for more than a second."

Wallis badly wanted to leave just then. His rule-of-thumb psychology was not working out, and because of his meddling Miss Murray was in a worse state now than when he had started. His well-intentioned lying had not come off, probably because it had been a ridiculous and *unbelievable* lie, the sort of lie which calls black white. Maybe if he had mixed a little more of the truth into it, cruel

78

though the truth was, the lie might have been believed. Or maybe not. But there was still time to try again.

"Well now," he said gently, "it seems that your scarred face bothers you. To be honest it bothers me, too, a little. But suppose I close one eye so as not to see your bad side. That way I'd be kissing one of the nicest-looking faces I've ever seen."

He cut short her objections by quickly smothering them, and this time he made sure that the kiss was not a hurried peck. It was like kissing the face of a marble statue, a cold and resilient marble face with imperfections on one side. She put her hand against his chest but did not push him away, and suddenly her arms were tight around him.

It was not a passionate embrace, Wallis thought, but more in the nature of the hug a frightened younger sister in need of protection gives to her big brother. It was not a passionate kiss, either, although her lips seemed to be softening and growing warmer. Through his open eye he could see that her face was relaxing, too, and becoming less strained. Maybe he wasn't such a bad psychologist after all, and it really was a small thing to do to make her feel better about things. Now if he counted up to ten slowly and then gently broke the near-stranglehold that she had on him, she certainly should not feel that this one had been a frightened peck.

There was a sudden, peculiar change in the expression in her face, an odd play of light and shade that made him think that there might be two sources of light in the tank instead of one. Wallis pulled away guiltily.

"I'll go out and come in again," said Dickson in a carefully neutral voice. He did just that, and then added, "Breakfast's ready, if anyone is interested."

XI

On the Unthan flagship the problems continued to be technical rather than personal. The food supply for the trip was ample if the crew spent practically all the time in Long Sleep, but completely inadequate for the needs of a small though increasing population who were continuously warm and drawing on it for many generations. Food would have to be grown, therefore, and while there was no shortage of the proper seed in the ship the growing of food required an increased temperature which, if the proper safety measures were not taken, could fatally affect the cooled passengers in the food-growing areas.

Fortunately, the flagship's crew were the best of the best, the top people in their particular specialties, so that purely technical problems did not worry them for long, but, for instance, both the organization and the transfer to tape and print of all the technical knowledge which allowed them to solve these problems did worry them, however, and continuously. It worried them even when all their records were complete and there was no longer any reason for them to remain warm in the ship.

The records of Hellahar and the captain were far from complete, partly because they had the rest of their lives in which to complete them and partly because their problems were more difficult of solution. Problems such as how to avoid a small-scale population explosion in the ship a few generations hence—a problem stemming from when the most important considerations in choosing the female section of the fleet had been the physical ability and a strong psychological urge to have children. And there were the more tenuous, but very real, personal problems that no amount of specialization or technical knowhow would help to solve, because the solutions were so intensely individual.

Deslann would have liked the crew to stay warm a little longer, if only to have their company and moral support. The healer was more honest about it, saying that the longer they were around, the farther off would be the evil hour when the captain and himself would have to start founding their dynasties. Meanwhile the crew had reached the point where they had nothing useful to do and were wasting precious biological time not doing it; so Deslann had a preliminary talk with the healer and then summoned them to the control room for the last time.

The last time, he silently corrected himself, so far as Hellahar and himself were concerned.

He made formal farewells, as did the healer, to each member of the crew, during which a great many informal things were said on each side. Deslann was surprised and deeply moved by the odd combination of insubordination and respect in some of the things they said. At the same time it was plainly obvious that they were afraid, afraid for themselves and for the thousands of others like them spread throughout the fleet. Afraid for their race and at the same time personally afraid that after they went into Long Sleep in a few minutes time they would never, never wake up.

There was little that Deslann could say that would make them feel better, but he had to try to say it.

He began, "The healer and myself will arrange, when the time comes, that you people will be warmed ahead of the other captain so that you will be able to explain the present situation to him and prepare him for what you will find when you are revived. I'm putting this badly, but that is because I have no real idea of what you will find then, only that it is sure to be a surprise.

"Of course, to look on the worst possible side of it," Deslann conjectured, "there is always the chance that our generations of captains and crews will mismanage things so badly that you will never be revived—that the pile will go critical or the timers will be damaged by unskilled maintenance or our descendants will kill each other off or die in some other fashion. Or you might waken to find that the fleet, or this ship or both, has missed the target sun and that there is nothing at all you can do about it."

This is supposed to be a pep-talk, Deslann reminded himself sharply; *you are not supposed to add all your own worries to theirs!*

"But I think that you can all rest contentedly," he resumed seriously, "because the possibilities I have just mentioned are extremely remote; perhaps they are impossibilities. Nobody knows better than yourselves the long, careful work which has gone into the recordings and training manuals for the use of the generations of astrogators, engineers, and computers to come. You can rest assured that the ship will be efficiently crewed and that you will reach the target system.

"After that . . ."

Deslann broke off, watching the faces of Gerrol and the others as they thought of what would happen after that. The truth was that none of them knew what would happen in detail, only that they would be close to a world that would be cool and almost completely covered by tremendous oceans, and that they would have to map and investigate those oceans and choose sites for the initial settlements, which must be at the correct depth and as free as possible from inimical life-forms, and that they must establish themselves securely enough and in enough time to guide in the main body of the fleet. The end of the journey might prove to be the most dangerous and difficult part as well as the most rewarding, and Deslann had fully expected to share both the dangers and the rewards. Now, though, he would share nothing except a lifetime of work and worry and hope that was so faint at times that it verged on outright self-deception.

There would be no rewards for Hellahar and himself or for a large number of the offspring still unborn. Not for the first time he felt a pang of sympathy for all the crews that were to come, and a sort of angry pity as he wondered if there ever could be enough hope, or self-deception, to balance the decades of unrewarding work ahead. His present crew did not know how lucky they were.

Very seriously, Deslann said, "We will not see each other again. You, on the other hand, will see each other in a very short time, because there is no detectable time lapse while in hibernation anesthesia. Of course, I don't know what sort of situation you will have to meet when you awaken. Doubtless there will be changes in language and customs and values, perhaps a certain amount of degeneration. To you, all these changes will seem to have happened within the next few minutes, so they will be bound to come as a shock. But no matter what that future crew has become or how it behaves, I would like you to treat them with sympathy and understanding. And respect.

"If for no other reason than that their ancestors were once your healer and your captain," he ended on a lighter note, repeating, "you will treat them with respect."

XII

The fight started over the use to which their remaining stock of oxygen tanks should be put. When *Gulf Trader* had begun to sink again the acetylene had given out and they had to use some of their oxygen. Dickson insisted that the next time they started to sink there was no point in keeping it afloat if they were going to suffocate anyway, while the doctor said that they were not really suffocating and must keep near the surface for as long as possible and hope for the best. Wallis got between them just in time.

They were both heavier men than he was, but he had been working with a length of heavy pipe when the argument started and so was able to negotiate from a position of strength. He told them that they probably would not be fighting if they had not been suffering from oxygen starvation and splitting headaches, but if they did not start behaving themselves their headaches would get much worse. They began to look ashamed of themselves and after that they never fought again, although they did argue nearly all the time.

The next time the ship became too still and quiet they used the oxygen tanks until the wave motion could be felt again. Half their original supply of tanked oxygen was gone and the air was becoming really foul. It was so bad that two people at a time were needed to work the generator and even then there had to be a third standing by with an oxygen tank in case one of them passed out. The two people not on the generator or standing by it stayed in the garden, where, with the lights in operation and the process of photosynthesis at work in the struggling young bean plants, the air was supposed to be fresher. It was hard to tell because everyone who stayed there for more than a few minutes needed nose plugs.

It was a day or night in the middle of June, while the girls were in the garden and the men were on the generator, when the subject of their air supply came up—not for the first time that day.

"Carbon dioxide is heavier than air," Radford said suddenly, "and the openings between the tanks are at the roof of each tank. Would it be possible to rig fans to keep the good air circulating so that—"

"They would blow that foul muck from Eleven and Twelve up here," Dickson broke in, "and we wouldn't be able to breathe at all, much less work the generator pedals."

"We need the generator," said Radford dully. "During daylight a plant absorbs CO_2 and releases oxygen. In darkness it releases excess CO_2 and produces no oxygen at all—"

"This intriguing horticultural fact," Dickson broke in, "has been mentioned by you before, Doctor. Also that the garden is doing well. But if this is the case, then why don't we feel the effects?"

"Because there is so much foul air down here in comparison with the leaf area of the beans!"

"You two gentlemen should step outside for a minute," Wallis said sharply. "Either that or change to a more pleasant subject."

Nobody laughed at the crack about stepping outside. They had all made it, and every conceivable variation on it, too many times for it to be funny anymore. Dickson continued pedaling in silence for several minutes, breathing deeply—hyperventilating, the doctor called it—before he replied.

"There is only one pleasant subject," he said, trying to look lascivious, "women. I can talk about them for hours. Not just the anatomical details, but the funny things they do sometimes. For instance, there's a certain female who doesn't live far away from here, who gets nervous and jumpy and cries a lot, and when a certain man, who also lives in the neighborhood, winks at her she stops being nervous and crying. It's a slow and, in my opinion—based on a wide experience of winking, ogling, and giving the eye generally—a meaningful wink. It is invariably given with the same eye and it is almost always effective.

"Curiosity," Dickson ended, "is killing me. And Jenny, and the doctor. . . ."

"Wild horses . . ." began Wallis, smiling to hide his embarrassment.

"I've thought of winking at her myself several times," Dickson went on quickly, "just to see if it works with other people. But she might misunderstand and Jenny *certainly* would not understand. And the doctor—"

" . . . Would have his name stricken from the rolls," Radford finished for him. "The BMA are very stuffy about patient-doctor relationships."

It was an odd situation, Wallis thought, especially as he had only kissed Margaret, with his eye closed, once. The effect on her seemed wildly out of proportion, because she appeared more often nowadays without her face bandages and when she was feeling bad, instead of talking to her and saying things which would merely make her feel embarrassed when the others were present, he would simply wink the eye on her bad side. He had thought about it a lot and had decided that her reaction was due partly to having a Big Secret to share with someone in a situation where privacy of any kind was practically nonexistent and partly to feeling that she was still attractive enough for someone to kiss her, if only once. And the trouble was that the secret had to be kept or the therapeutic wink, as the doctor called it, would lose its effect.

Dickson, still trying desperately to satisfy his curiosity, changed his line of attack.

"It seems to me that people who wink at people," he went on, still lasciviously, "are indulging in a form of, uh, intimacy—the early stages of intimacy, of course. I'm talking about winking between men people and women people at the moment, as I don't want to get sidetracked onto the subject of fairy-type people."

"I'm glad," said Wallis.

"Such intimacy should not be indulged," Dickson continued unchecked, "by an officer or a gentleman, or both, unless his intentions are honorable. It could be argued that continued winking is tantamount to having an 'understanding,' or being unofficially engaged. However, the problems of a couple engaged to be married are many, and require a certain amount of tact and—"

"My intentions aren't—I mean, I don't *have* intentions!" Wallis protested, almost laughing.

"Requiring tact and understanding from those who are already married and have experienced and surmounted these difficulties," Dickson went on as if Wallis hadn't spoken. "The first problem may be that of the marriage itself, which turns out to be the easiest of all, since as a first officer with a master's ticket, and bearing in mind the fact that in the merchant service we marry people at sea much more frequently than they do in the Royal Navy, I would be glad to officiate and return the favor already done me. A simple case of you marry me and I'll marry you. Not *you*, of course—I mean the two of you."

"I understand," said Wallis.

"The next difficulty," Dickson resumed, "may be that of ignorance. The complete or partial ignorance regarding, uh, geography and, uh, technique. I mean, there's this business with the birds and the bees—"

"I kept rabbits as a boy," said Wallis gravely, "and my stern old father told me about people."

"Good!" said Dickson. "You have a grounding in birds, bees, rabbits, and people. You understand the subtle urge—nothing to be ashamed of, mind!—which brings the two sexes together. What you perhaps do not fully appreciate is the purely physical problem, a problem which normally does not exist with bees and rabbits and even people, of bringing them together closely enough when in so doing for a single unguarded movement or carelessness in arranging the sacking could let in a blast of cold air which would certainly ruin the warm, tender, and romantic atmosphere it is one's intention to create and which might result in pneumonia or rheumatism besides—"

"Where do you find the breath," said Wallis, wanting suddenly to change the subject again, "to pedal and talk at the same time?"

"It isn't because of fresh air and exercise," the doctor said, adding, "or, I suspect, from clean living."

Ignoring them both, Dickson went on delicately, "My own hard-won experience in this matter may be of interest, and possibly of value to you. To begin with we shall assume that the two people of opposite, uh, gender are under their heap of sacking and that the psychological climate is right, that there will be mutual cooperation during the forthcoming project. The problems which then remain are basically those concerning clothing, the need for operating in a confined space in darkness, and the necessity for silence so as to avoid the embarrassment of people. . . ." He looked pointedly at the doctor, " . . . making cracks at breakfast time. The first thing you must do. . . ."

Dickson went into detail regarding the first thing, the second thing, and the third thing. He spoke quietly and gravely, and if his tongue was in his cheek the fact was not at all obvious. When he had dealt with the fifteenth or sixteenth, and last, thing, it was the doctor who broke the ensuing silence.

"Better change the subject again, Dickson," he said, smiling. "I think you're making the commander feel uncomfortable."

"The word," said Wallis, "is overstimulated."

A few days later it became impossible to talk while at the generator, and gradually it became the accepted thing for one or other of them to black out while pedaling and need to be revived with pure oxygen. The only comfortable place was in the garden when the lights were on, but then only two of them could use it at a time. The most uncomfortable time was the period between sleeping and working the generator, when they had nothing to do but think and when they thought so much that it was nearly impossible to sleep at all.

They all breathed too fast and sweated despite the cold and snapped at each other for nothing at all. At first Wallis had tried to use his authority to stop this continual bickering, but he had a constant, thudding headache which soured his every waking minute and which throbbed in the background of his dreams, and more often than not he found himself snapping and snarling as badly as the rest of them. By far the worst offender was Margaret Murray, who had begun to have waking nightmares about her time on the raft again and who had begun to cry all the time and cover her burnt face again despite all that Wallis could do. In the doctor's opinion Wallis wasn't doing enough.

"Your winking isn't having much effect these days," he told Wallis on an occasion when they were alone in the garden together. "Whatever it was that you did to make a wink have such good results—well, to put it bluntly, sir, she needs a booster shot."

Wallis had to administer several booster shots, because the law of diminishing returns seemed to have come into force in this particular situation. But the medicine was pleasant to administer so he did not mind. He felt, in fact, that it would have been very pleasant indeed if it had not been for the frigid, stinking air, which gave them headaches that threatened to blow the tops off their skulls and which made them pull away gasping desperately for breath after a kiss lasting only a few seconds. Dickson discovered them several times in what he was fond of describing as a compromising situation and as many times suggested that somebody should make an honest woman out of someone. The doctor, however, was strongly against this, for the time being anyway. He said that they should all remain as calm as possible and should not indulge in any strenuous activity, other than on the generator, which might waste oxygen. . . .

Being able to breathe became much more important than feeling warm. Radford and Wallis, and even the Dicksons, split up during the so-called sleep periods. Perhaps it was a psychological thing, but they felt too stifled under their shared heaps of sacking. So they slept alone with their faces uncovered and their breaths puffing up into the darkness as if they were so many steam locomotives. It was nearly impossible to sleep. All they could do was lie and gasp for breath, and think.

"I've been thinking," said Wallis one "night" toward the end of July. "On lifeboats we hear of people singing and playing games to keep awake. Our problem is not to stay awake but to keep from going stark raving mad because we can't sleep."

He stopped to catch his breath and then went on, "In one way the situation is the same. We have to exercise our minds so as not to dwell too much on our surroundings. Physical exercise is out, but there's nothing to stop our exercising our brains. I had in mind a sort of quiz."

"Talking uses oxygen," said Dickson. "Besides, we already know how each other's minds work. We've talked about ourselves often enough."

"I'm not so sure that talking wastes all that much oxygen," the doctor said. "In any case the mental benefits outweigh the extra risk if the quiz game really takes our minds off our physical discomfort. Provided we don't shout or get excited, it should be okay. But I must forbid singing for the time being."

"Pity!" said Margaret Murray. "I'm a top soprano."

"Me, too," said Jenny Dickson. "And I don't much like quiz games."

"I'm a Gilbert and Sullivan man myself," the doctor joined in. "In the school operatic society I was Pooh-Bah one year, and another time I understudied the Lord Chancellor in *Iolanthe*."

"You never told us *that*," said Dickson accusingly. "I would have let you hear me do 'Frankie and Johnny.' "

"All this is news to me, too," said Wallis firmly, "but I must repeat that singing is out for the time being. And it seems plain that we *don't* know everything about each other as yet. Also, if this game works out the way I'd like it to, we will do very little talking and a great deal of thinking, so that the oxygen wastage will be negligible. . . ."

The questions in this quiz game would not be easy, Wallis went on to explain. They would, in fact, be next to impossible. The game would begin by each of them being set a memory test. Something like "How much can you remember about your eleventh birthday party?" or "What was in the last Sunday paper you read, besides pin-ups?" Later the questions would become more difficult, such as how much could be remembered of a particular chapter in a particular book or how much could be recalled of a certain day in the past chosen completely at random. They would each tell what, if anything, they could remember regarding their individual tests, then they would go back repeatedly and go over the memory again and again until it was as complete and detailed as possible. At intervals they would report progesss on their particular assignments, but, as they could see, most of the time would be spent thinking.

Radford joined in at that point to say that many psychologists believed that no memory was ever lost, that memories were allowed to fade but could be recalled in their entirety by patient and persistent questioning. That they would be asking the questions of themselves made no essential difference. The girls, Dickson, and Wallis himself suggested modifications to the game and they talked about it for a very long time, so much so that they began to fall asleep before they actually got around to playing it.

The next "night" they started playing the game, awkwardly and self-consciously at first. But very soon the Game took a firm hold on them—it was competitive, endless, difficult and nobody either won or lost. During the early part of their sleep period it was normal for them all to lie still and silent, breathing and thinking hard, but not thinking, or worrying, about breathing.

But the air became steadily more foul. The generator was operated by one of them at a time, using a jury-rigged oxygen tent fed by their steadily diminishing store of tanked gas, while the others stayed in the relatively fresh air of the garden, which now covered most of the floor of Number Three. At "night" the Game helped, but still they struggled awake, shouting and kicking, from nightmares of drowning or worse. They all did this, the girls a little more often than the men. The worst part of it was that when they did wake they still felt as if they were choking to death.

It became impossible to sleep at night, so they slept in the garden during the electrically lit "day" instead, passing the night by playing the Game. This helped everyone for a while, until the ship began to sink once more, and once more the angry, bitter arguments raged over whether they should use their remaining oxygen to reduce depth or keep it to breathe and have the hull cave in on

91

them, whether to die of asphyxiation through carbon-dioxide poisoning or through simple drowning.

Then the hull began to emit creaking sounds, very soft as yet, and a sort of loud, metallic sighing. *Gulf Trader* was beginning to break up.

XIII

It was an incredibly slow process, so slow that they had time to get over their private or public panic and settle down merely to listen to the ship breaking up all around them—though, to be quite accurate, most of the noises seemed to be coming from the stern and the others may have been reverberations.

With the irregular sighing noises aft there came the grinding and the hollow, underwater screaming sounds of tearing metal, also irregular but increasing in frequency. They could feel the deck shuddering under them even through the sacking. The grinding and tearing seemed to go on for hours.

"This is going to take a long time," said the doctor suddenly. "The air would be . . . fresher in the garden with the generator going. Lying here just listening is . . . making me feel morbid."

"The salt water will ruin your crops," said Dickson. Jenny was hanging onto him tightly and looked ready to cry again, so he probably felt obliged to make a crack to keep up her morale, or both their morales. Wallis was holding Margaret Murray's hand, and she was holding his so tightly that his fingers ached, but he could not think of anything smart or cheerful to say.

"I wonder why all the noise is coming from the stern," he said. "We're down by the stern, but not more than twenty or thirty feet and that . . . isn't enough to make a big . . . pressure difference. The engine room took a hit, so the hull is weak there, . . . but so did the bow, and nothing is happening for'rard."

A few seconds after he had stopped talking there was a tearing crash from the bows and the sound was repeated at short intervals, seeming to come closer along their starboard side. With each crash the deck shook and the

93

Trader began a definite list to port. It was easy to imagine the steadily mounting pressure finding weak points in the hull where the two torpedoes had struck, then slowly squeezing open the hull along the line of one of the longitudinal welds. There was another crash for'ard and grinding, tearing sounds marched remorselessly towards them, this time along the port side.

"You and your big mouth," said Dickson, quickly adding, "sir."

They lay waiting for the tank walls to buckle inward and for the crushing weight of water to smash down on them, spin them about, and thrust its way into their straining lungs. The din around them reached a crescendo, but still the walls held, and there was no sound of water flooding through the holds even when the crashing began to die down. Wallis, who had been gripping Margaret's hand as tightly toward the end as she had been gripping his, pried open her fingers and felt around for the torch. When he switched it on he saw that the walls of the tank were still bone dry. A few minutes later after a single and relatively soft crash the ship became silent and still again.

"You know," said Wallis, in a voice which was nearly falsetto with joy, "I don't think we're sinking at all! I think we've run aground!"

They did not believe him at first, but then they considered the facts in the shape of the recent crashes, creaks, and bumps in conjunction with this new theory and found that they fitted it very well. *Trader* might very easily have drifted under the influence of tide or current onto a gently sloping bottom, the stern touching first so that the ship had swung around to continue the drift bow first. The shelving bottom must have been sandy, judging by the earlier sighing sounds, but with many outcroppings of rock. The more dramatic noises must have been caused by plating loosened by the torpedo astern being pulled off as the ship touched bottom, and later by the hull drifting over or alongship rocks. Eventually the ship had come to rest—at high tide, presumably, because there were no later indications that she would drift off—and jammed herself solidly onto a sea bed whose slope followed the original

, an hour or a day—at a time. It would begin by [v]im's being asked to remember all that he or she [?] regarding a date in his past chosen at random, [?] was usually nothing at all, at first. But then the [?] four would question the victim closely until some [?] fact would be remembered, and they would persist, [?] ays if necessary, until the memories of that tiny seg[ment] of his lifetime were recovered intact. The process [?] leave both the victim and interrogators feeling more [?] out than if they had just come off a long stint on [?] generator, so that the Game helped them to sleep as [?]

[S]ometimes the memories being sought involved the [v]ictim's recounting conversations he or she had held or had [ov]erheard, and on these occasions he or she was expected [to] fully describe the people concerned and to do his or her [be]st at reproducing voices and mannerisms. The inter[r]ogators would have run the victim through the incident [s]o many times that they would know it as well as the [v]ictim did. Very often, too, they would end by each of [t]hem playing the part and performing the actions of one of the characters in the memory, a memory which a short time previously the victim had not even known he possessed.

It was no great effort to remember the dramatic incident's in one's life, so the main interest and fun of the Game was in bringing up the normal, ordinary events: such as Dickson's memory of the twelfth of April, 1935, between four and five in the afternoon, when he had arrived home from school. Margaret had played his mother talking to his father, the doctor, while Wallis had played his younger brother and Jenny, who was an extremely good mimic, had been the radio going in the living room. [S]ometimes they went over funny or pleasant easy-to-remember incidents merely for the sake of entertainment. [O]ccasionally the doctor would get off on his own pet [p]roject of trying to make them remember, word for word, [s]ome of the books they had read. They had all considered [t]his to be impossible, at first, but when Wallis found him[s]elf reciting long sequences from *Alice in Wonderland* they [b]egan to have second thoughts.

98

stern-down attitude of the ship so closely that to those inside there was no detectable difference.

"We're very lucky," said the doctor.

"Maybe we were all born to be hanged," said Margaret.

"That's still too close to asphyxiation for comfort," said Dickson. "Couldn't we be born to die in bed?"

So they went back to working the generator one at a time while the others stayed in the garden. Then sometime in mid-August Dickson found that he could pedal for a considerable time without the bulky oxygen tent, and very soon they did not need oxygen at all. Once again they could walk the length of the ship without discomfort and they could sleep without dreaming that they were choking to death. They still had eight tanks of oxygen and one of acetylene, which had been overlooked in the general confusion, to hold against possible emergencies.

The doctor's garden was a success.

But for some reason the doctor seemed more angry than pleased when they tried to praise him. And it was not until after Wallis had asked the first mate and acting-captain (of the merchant service) to perform the nuptial ceremony and had been married and excused from generator detail and the Game for a three-day honeymoon that Wallis discovered the reason for the doctor's anger. They were alone at the time in Seven, working on another distillation apparatus, and Wallis had just tried again to compliment the surgeon lieutenant on the success of his garden.

"I thought it would work," Radford said angrily, "but I didn't think there was enough time. I thought we would all be dead and on the bottom by now. Instead we have food and water and air, and we're alive!"

"Is that bad?" said Wallis, smiling.

"It isn't altogether good," said the doctor sharply. "There are complications when people stay alive. One of them— well, let's say that one of our biological clocks has stopped."

"Oh," said Wallis.

"Yes," said the doctor. "It isn't to be mentioned to anyone yet, you understand. They don't feel very well about it. This isn't the sort of place to bring a kid into the world. In fact it's about the worst place I know of for the baby

95

and its mother, and the parents realize it. You can be sure it wasn't deliberate, but under the circumstances . . ." He shrugged angrily and bent over the workbench again.

"I understand your feelings," Wallis said seriously. "But you're an even better doctor, Doctor, than you are a gardener."

"You think you understand," said Radford, who then went on to detail some of the preparations and problems involved in having a confinement in the dark, frigid hold of a sunken ship with no medical facilities except a few rolls of adhesive plaster. It was with great difficulty that Wallis got him off that subject and onto ideas for improving the interior of their living quarters and the comfort of the ship generally.

Despite the many odd jobs and major alterations which had to be done, they still had too much time with nothing at all to do, and there were times when bordom became such a crushing, smothering weight that it affected them much as the foul air had done in earlier days. Plainly the only answer was to increase the scope of the Game. There were many possibilities now that there was air and they could talk and jog each other's memories and perform various psychological tricks instead of lying silent and thinking most of the time. But when Wallis was with Margaret that night the original subject came up again.

He had brought it up himself, but without mentioning the Dicksons, and had talked all around the subject, and was beginning to go round again in his efforts not to say anything which would give offense. After all, they had been married for just three days—three "days" and four sleeping periods to be exact—and he was on dangerous ground.

"I don't think this is a place to have a baby, either," Margaret said when he had finally bogged down. "Nobody in their right mind would consider it for a minute. But there have been times, these past few days, when neither of us was in his right mind—at least, I know *I* wasn't. What I mean is, it's going to be very hard not to . . . to . . ."

"Practically impossible," said Wallis softly.

"Yes," she said, and sighed. "But you brought the

subject up, you know, not me. Did [ ] some sort of answer, in mind?"

"Well," said Wallis lightly, "there [ ] heaps of sacking."

"You *beast*!"

"I was joking," said Wallis quickly.

He felt her body stiffen in his arms a[ ] she lay silent, then suddenly she rela[ ] close.

"Close that eye," she said, "and kiss me.[ ]

The complicated techniques evolved by [ ] for getting together were no longer quite so [ ] the temperature had risen in the ship until i[ ] fortably cool rather than unbearably cold. S[ ] and possible warm currents were the probable [ ] there were periodic increases in temperature, [ ] undoubtedly caused by the ebb-tide flowing [ ] sun-warmed sand or rocks. The ship's interio[ ] come a relatively comfortable place by mid-Se[ ] with the generator and garden and distillation gea[ ] ing well—so much so that Dickson volunteered for, [ ] actually took, the first bath.

He did it just to please the doctor, Dickson told [ ] one, and not because his best friends were telling him[ ]

Despite the many improvements made in their [ ] quarters and the projects which Dickson, the docto[ ] Wallis were always working on, there was not eno[ ] do in the ship to keep their minds occupied. They h[ ] idea where they were, although Wallis thought tha[ ] might have drifted as far south as the coast of Fra[ ] Spain, and they had not heard a ship's engines s[ ] month before they had run aground. Their chances o[ ] detected and rescued were vanishingly small, and [ ] so as not to think about this that they played [ ] culiar mixture of parlor psychology and medieval [ ] tion which was the Game.

Apart from the Handbook of Marine Engi[ ] Part One, and a number of greasy blueprints th[ ] nothing to read on the ship, so that the Game had [ ] a method of reading each other a page—or [ ]

It was almost frightening how good their memories had become, and how much the Game had come to mean to them.

December came and the water lost the last of its stored summer heat. With *Alice* complete the doctor was digging happily into the minds of Dickson and Wallis for *Julius Caesar*, in which they both had had parts when they were at school. Meanwhile they were simultaneously squeezing *Madame Butterfly* out of Margaret. It was also the time when, in the words of Dickson, his wife was more beautiful than ever but definitely pear-shaped, and it was the time when the second biological clock stopped.

When Wallis told him about it the doctor swore horribly and would not speak to anyone for the rest of the day.

XIV

"There is absolutely no reason for you to worry," said Hellahar, when they were alone together between examinations. The healer went on, "You must know, sir, that the ship has all the necessary medical and surgical resources, in this field especially. After all, the fleet is basically a colonization project, even though there will be no mother world when the colony is planted, and the medical problems attached to giving birth have received special attention."

"I know," said Deslann.

"There is also the fact," Hellahar went on, "which if I were a modest person I would not mention, that I am an unusually able healer. You must remember this is a natural, if rather painful, process and the danger to the mother and child is minimal."

"I know that, too," said Deslann. "There is no logical reason for my concern, much less for me to be tying my tail in knots over it. The process has been going on for millions of years. I've nothing to worry about. But suppose it was your child about to be born instead of mine, what then?"

"When that time comes," the healer replied gravely, "I would appreciate it if you would tell me all the things I'm now telling you, and try just as hard to make me believe them. . . ."

On *Gulf Trader* there was ability and knowledge but the medical resources were practically nonexistent. There wasn't even an adequate supply of hot water. What little there was had been produced by Wallis inserting the flame of the oxyacetylene welder into buckets of sea water (the garden was doing so well that they could afford to burn a little oxygen) and holding it there until the water boiled.

But mostly he worked on the generator. In fact, all, with the exception of the expectant mother and the doctor, worked on the generator longer and harder than they had ever done before. They desperately needed the light.

It was a long and difficult confinement, Radford admitted later, although at the time and to Jenny he swore himself blind that everything was in all respects normal. But their troubles were not over even when the baby was finally detached from its mother and had had the soles of her feet slapped until she complained loudly about it. In the special crib they had rigged, which was kept warm with improvised hot-water bottles and heated further (and almost burned in places) by Wallis waving his acetylene torch along the blankets, the baby started to turn blue and had to be given oxygen. They had to use one of the tanks from the welder and in the confusion nearly gave it acetylene by mistake. By the time the baby was taken care of its mother needed oxygen as well and was going into shock.

She was so slow to respond that that night Dickson and Margaret slept on either side of Jenny with their arms around her and their bodies pressed close to give her warmth. It was the doctor's suggestion, and if Dickson thought of making any cracks about sleeping with two women at the same time, for once he kept them to himself.

Much later, when Jenny and her baby were as comfortable as circumstances permitted and Wallis and the doctor were sitting shivering in the darkness a short distance away, an odd, low-voiced conversation started up. The surgeon lieutenant seemed to be afflicted with a fit of the verbal shakes and could not stop talking, while Wallis tried to thank and compliment him for what he had done. But he was so cold and tense himself that he did not make a very good job of it.

"You were very good, Doctor," he said quickly, during a break. "I . . . I was surprised how . . . how messy it was. I had no idea . . ."

"Of course not," said Radford. "Wouldn't expect it. But there's nothing for you to worry about. Except that you might ask Margaret to think about kangaroos. She designed these coveralls and they're very good. Papoose carriers, I

101

mean. And slung in front instead of at the back. For ease of feeding, you understand, as well as warmth. The place is too damned cold to leave a baby lying around. And we'll have to excuse Jenny from the generator for a while. Margaret, too, she's getting heavy. Any twins in your family?"

"No," said Wallis, "but . . ."

"Don't worry, anyway," said the doctor. "This was a bad one, it would have been tricky even in a hospital. Yours should come much more easily. Especially as we have a better idea of the drill, now. Don't worry, the next one will be comparatively easy."

"You sound," said Wallis, "as if you're looking forward to it."

Radford was silent for a long time, but when he spoke again his tone and manner were back to normal. He said, "I didn't mean to give that impression, sir. If I did it's because I've been hanging on to my bedside manner for so long that I've forgotten to let go even with you. But this has been a difficult birth, so much so that your wife would have to be very unfortunate indeed to have one as bad. This is fact based on examination and what medical history there is available, not just a pep-talk for a worried parent-to-be. And in any event I will do everything possible to—"

"We know you will, Doctor," said Wallis. "Believe me, we're not worried about *that*. . . ."

"Perhaps not," said the doctor grimly, "but I *am* worried. More accurately, I'm scared stiff. And I'll be doing my best for more than the usual reasons—Hippocratic oath, medical ethics, and so on. The truth is that I can't allow anyone to die on me. The very thought of it gives me nightmares. In this place, what could we do with the body?"

Wallis was unable to answer the question then or later, when the doctor had fallen into an exhausted sleep sitting up, or even when he thought about it during odd moments in the weeks which followed. It was not a nice question, and trying to think of an answer started a train of thought which was usually too horrible to be completed. Especially when it involved Margaret. The thought of her being dead was bad enough. But for her to be dead and close by all the time, with the processes of decay going on. They would probably put her in some out-of-the-way corner of a tank, in a tool locker, perhaps, with cargo piled around it to mask off the smell. But she would still be there and everyone would know it. For Wallis it would be a parting which was not a parting and he did not think that he could stand it.

Like the doctor, Wallis had quite a few nightmares and woke with Margaret holding him tightly and stroking his head as if he were a baby. She wanted to know what was the matter and he could not tell her; all he could do was hold her as tightly as she was holding him. Again like the doctor, he learned how not to think about it and to pretend that it could never happen.

The Game suffered because Jenny wanted them to be quiet so as to let the baby sleep, and their own sleep was interrupted because the baby decided to wake up again at the wrong time. Despite himself it made Wallis furious. Getting to sleep was difficult at the best of times and he looked on it as a most desirable condition, since it was only during sleep that he could forget the cold metal of their prison with its deadly monotony of unwarmed food and pedaling the generator and trying not to go insane from sheer boredom. During sleep he could dream of things like eating porridge and hot stew or just drinking tea all night long. It was odd how the dishes never were fancy or exotic, they were simply warm. And when the wailings and whimperings of the recently arrived Geraldine Elizabeth Dickson started up, Wallis gritted his teeth and tried vainly to hang onto his lovely warm dreams and felt like murder.

The care and feeding of the new arrival was a complicated business in many ways.

"Basically it's a problem of keeping the thing warm without smothering it to death," the doctor said on an occasion when the men were in the generator room together, "especially when it's being changed—which brings up another point. We've given it all the blankets and slapped the squares of sacking in use for nappies . . ."

"Diapers," said Dickson.

103

". . . against the plating until they are not only dry but nearly as soft as cotton wool. But this doesn't satisfy the maternal instinct. The girls insist that the nappies are damp and harsh against its skin. I keep telling them what the Spartans used to do with babies, but . . ."

"They are things you put on your lap in a restaurant, Doctor," said Dickson firmly, "or tuck into your collar if you're uncouth."

". . . it doesn't get me anywhere," Radford went on, disregarding him. "Admittedly there is some chafing of the skin, but all things considered it is a very healthy child and there's no need for all the complaining. About the only thing they don't complain about is the feeding of the child. That particular process is the same here as anywhere else and is relatively uncomplicated."

"So far, Doctor," said Dickson, grinning; "what bothers me is how we are going to wean it off mother's milk and onto cold powdered-egg soup—"

"This is serious!" Wallis broke in irritably. "There is too much complaining and too much fuss generally about the baby. Morale is suffering. We're being too damned quiet for our own good and thinking too much about all the wrong things! With respect to your daughter, Dickson, I think she should learn to sleep with a certain amount of talk going on around her. I myself have a nephew who can sleep for hours in the same room as a wireless going full blast—"

"Radio," corrected Dickson automatically.

"It's a good idea, sir," Radford said quickly, seeing the commander's expression. Wallis had very little sense of humor these days, and even less patience, as Margaret's time came steadily nearer. The doctor added, "We've all missed playing the Game, sir. Even the girls . . ."

The nursery on the flagship was a small compartment whose water was maintained at close to blood temperature and whose walls, ceiling, and floor, except for the small area covered by the transparent observation panel, were lined with soft, spongy plastic so that the two tiny beings darting about the interior with nearly mindless violence would not injure themselves.

"Look at him go!" said Hellahar excitedly. "Did you

104

ever see such a healthy child! You know, without wishing to seem boastful, and making due allowance for paternal pride, I really do think that he is one of the nicest and most physically perfect male young 'uns that ever was born!"

"I agree," said Deslann, "provided you admit that mine is one of the nicest females. . . ."

Above and beyond *Gulf Trader* the war was over, conventionally in Europe and then a little later in Japan in such a fashion that the world would never feel completely safe again. But inside the ship they very rarely talked about the war. They had been withdrawn from it at a very critical period and, while they hoped and believed their side would win, they had no way of knowing for sure. Another reason was that three years or more of the Game had so developed their faculties for recalling sights and sounds and people that they did not even want to think about it, because there was very little in the wartime memories of any of them which was pleasant.

During this period the improvements in the comfort and appearance of the tanks were minor, inasmuch as there was only a limited amount of insulating and building material and as the doctor did not want them to use too much of the paint supply because of the danger from the fumes in the confined space. They heard ships passing, but in the distance and not very often, so they gradually stopped signaling. Banging with crowbars against the hull plating, besides frightening the children, made them all start thinking about the wrong things again, even though everyone knew that the *right* things were the current Game project of ways to improve the Game itself.

With nothing to do for three-quarters of each and every day except sleep and talk and think—and sleeping did not seem to take up as much time as it ought—they should have gone stark staring mad during the first six months out of sheer boredom. Wallis had encountered a character in a science fiction story once who had said that if a person were to study one single fact or object for a long enough period of time the complete structure of the Universe could eventually be deduced from it. In *Gulf Trader* they had time and many facts and occasionally they even dis-

105

cussed the nature of the Universe, but the big thing was that they had been left very much to their own mental devices and had not gone mad. If anything, the doctor affirmed, they were going steadily more sane—although just recently he himself was not behaving in any sort of adult, logical manner.

Currently they were engaged in digging for French, the idea being that when the data from all their school-days memories, sayings, and snippets of overheard conversations and so on were assembled they would speak only French to each other for a few weeks, just as they had done with Latin a few months back. The children were building things with empty powdered-egg tins and knocking them down again, but they were three tanks away so that the noise was not distracting, and the doctor was pedaling silently while the others talked. Perhaps unconsciously they had been digging around in the memories of French grammar and pronunciation and similar school-days material, so that it was not a surprise to anyone when they wandered off the subject, as often happened, and onto another which would eventually form a future Game project—that of educating the children.

Except for the doctor, who had the breath to speak if he wanted to despite the pedaling, they all had a great deal to say about the subject. But it was Wallis who pointed out an aspect of it which had not yet been considered, that of religious education.

"How much of it we teach," Wallis offered, "and the form it takes rather depends on what we ourselves feel about it. We might teach only the basics without going too deeply into any particular religion. But it's a touchy subject. Does anyone here have strong feelings in the matter?"

The doctor held some strong views on this subject, although he did not as a rule try to ram his own beliefs down anyone else's throat; so the question should have roused him if anything would, but he continued pedaling in silence. It was Margaret who spoke first.

"I haven't read all the Bible," she said, "but there are the Commandments, everybody believes in them—"

"And the opening questions and answers in the Chil-

106

dren's Catechism," Jenny broke in. "I can remember most of them without digging, even. It starts like this. Question: Who made the world?"

"Answer," said her husband. "The Brooklyn Navy Yard."

"Dickson," said the doctor sharply, breaking a silence which had lasted since the moment two days ago when he discovered that both of his biological clocks had stopped again, "don't be so blasted irreverent!"

XV

In another corner of the same ocean records were being broken and great deeds were being done. One of the new nuclear submarines, bigger and more powerful and capable of diving to a greater depth than any conventional submarine, had astonished the world by running submerged and completely cut off from all contact with the surface for two whole months. Had they known about this the inhabitants of *Gulf Trader* might have felt a certain amount of justifiable smugness. But they did not know, and while the crew of that fantastic vessel were being given the freedom of the city for their exploit and already beginning to talk in terms of circumnavigating the world submerged and/or sailing under the North Pole as an encore, the people in *Trader* were relaxing after a stiff session of the Game by talking about anything at all which came into their heads.

"It was nice of you two," said the doctor, looking at Dickson and Wallis, "to arrange your families the way you did. A boy and a girl each. Considerate."

"Think nothing of it," said Wallis.

"It was a pleasure," said Dickson.

"If you hadn't been so thoughtful," Radford went on, "we might have had polygamy raising its ugly head, or that other thing where there are more men than women——"

"A fate worse than death," murmured Dickson.

". . . but even as things stand," the doctor went on, ignoring him, "we will have to do some thinking about our respective medical histories. All of us here have passed the Service entrance medicals so we know that we are reasonably healthy specimens, but I'm more interested in the ailments of our ancestors—especially in hereditary diseases they may have suffered, like hemophilia or leukemia, or TB or . . ." he looked pointedly at Dickson ". . . insanity. The coming generation is all right, but with the next one there will be inbreeding to consider.

"Or maybe I'm thinking too far ahead," he ended awkwardly.

On the other side of the tank the children were playing a game of their own, quietly and almost surreptitiously for them. Wallis recognized enough of the whispered dialogue to suspect that the adults would shortly be treated to a new full-scale production of *Snow White,* with Gerry Dickson in the name part, Eileen Wallis as the Wicked Queen, and Dave Wallis and Joe Dickson sharing the other seven parts between them. They seemed to be improvising quite a lot on the original theme.

To the doctor, the lieutenant commander said, "No, I don't think so. It's a funny thing, but I find myself thinking more and more often that this place is the normal, everyday world and the real world on the surface is something we know by hearsay, like material in a book dug up during the Game—"

"Speaking of books and the Game," the doctor put in, "I was wondering if it wouldn't be a good thing to specialize more. Instead of all of us helping to remember a book or a play, have each of us remember something he or she has read, but doing it solo and then talking it out on request. There are a lot of things that we have read or done which are not common to the others. I think we are good enough at remembering now to be able to do that.

"I myself have read the Hornblower trilogy five times," he went on, "so that I could start with those stories."

"I read *The Happy Return* once," Margaret said. "Just once. I didn't understand the technical bits, but I loved Hornblower. He was a nice, understanding, worried sort of hero for a change, with thinning hair and skinny, too. I really felt for that man."

"Faithless hussy," said Dickson.

"The Hornblower stories resemble science fiction in many ways," said Wallis. "They show the past rather than the future, of course, but they describe a slightly alien world whose language and technology require a certain amount of effort to understand, and the effort increases the enjoyment.

109

"But I'm not an authority on Forester," Wallis added quickly, seeing the doctor's suddenly glum expression. "I've read only *A Ship of the Line* and that only once, so I'd be glad to hear the first and third books, Doctor, if you can dig them out of your brain. The only story which I have read anything like five times was by a Dr. Smith—not a *real* doctor, Doctor, just a Ph.D.—who, as well as stretching my imagination to its elastic limit, had horrible alien beings who were actually good 'uns instead of being utterly and completely hostile.

"There have been other stories with the same idea—better written, perhaps," Wallis continued enthusiastically. "I picked up a few of them during my last stopover in New York. But that particular one was my first experience of science fiction and it has stuck with me—especially a character in it who was a winged dragon with scales, claws, four extensible eyes, and a lot of other visually horrifying features and who was more human than some of the human characters. There were bad 'uns, too, of course; I can remember a piece of the opening chapter which goes . . ."

He closed his eyes for a moment, bringing back an image that was partly the sound of words, partly the memory of the printed page, and partly the picture which both of them described; then he recited, " 'Among the world-girdling fortifications of a planet distant indeed from star cluster AG-257-4736 there squatted sullenly a fortress quite similar to Helmuth's own. . . . It was cold and dark withal, for its occupants had practically nothing in common with humanity save the possession of high intelligence. . . .' Uh, let's see . . . yes. . . . 'It was not exactly like an octopus. Nor, although it was scaly and toothy and wingy, was it, save in the vaguest possible way, similar to a sea serpent, a lizard, or a vulture. . . .' "

"I don't think many people here could have read *that* story," said Dickson, when Wallis began to bog down. There was a touch of awe in his tone.

"Yes indeed," said the doctor, "I'd like to hear more of it."

"Not until the children have gone to bed," said Margaret firmly. "I don't want them frightened to death!"

But as time went on the children, who seemed to grow older and more inquisitive with incredible rapidity, were not unduly disturbed by anything they overheard. Wallis had read, and was eventually able to remember, a great many stories other than science fiction, and in addition there was the technical knowledge acquired learning his profession. The same applied to the material, both fact and fiction, recalled by the doctor and Dickson and even the girls. Singing was still a better form of entertainment than listening to stories—music did not suffer so much with repetition—although a song or an operetta did not give as much food for discussion afterwards. And the children, listening to descriptions of the stars and navigation and Jenny's *Ranch Romances* and passages from Gray's *Anatomy* or *Gray Lensman,* were excited and curious and just a little bit bored by it all.

"You have to realize," said the doctor, after they had discussed just this point for several hours and some of them were still feeling worried about it, "that practically everything we tell them is secondhand. Deep down they may doubt that such things as dogs and cities and forests exist. It is very difficult to describe the whole world in words alone, and the models and pictures we've tried to produce are not really adequate.

"As well," he went on, "at their particular age-group they are physically and mentally restless. They want to do things with the knowledge they have learned, and it is bound to take a while for them to realize, like their parents, that the only long-term activity available to them here is mental activity. . . ."

But the adjustment of using the mind for the greater part of every day rather than their young and, in the circumstances, surprisingly healthy bodies was not an easy one for adolescents to make. There was trouble—quarreling and nagging and even an odd fist-fight, in which the fond, irritated or at times downright angry parents could not help but become embroiled—which lasted for the best part of five years. But the children married young, thus helping to stabilize things considerably. All except Richard Dickson, the third child and second son of that family.

Margaret and the commander did not produce another

daughter, or a son either, for that matter, so it looked as if young Richard was going to be a bachelor. Both professionally and personally the doctor was not in favor of Margaret's having any more children, and they had all absorbed enough of his medical diggings to appreciate the reasons. But he was at great pains to reassure Richard's parents that doing without female company was not a thing to be worried about, that he entirely disagreed with Freud and such people about the effects of sexual frustration, and that he himself was a case in point. Admittedly he was a little grumpy and hard to get on with at times, but this was due to his being a naturally mean and bad-tempered person. Dickson immediately agreed with him.

But young Richard was mean and bad-tempered all the time.

On the Unthan flagship the time passed and the population and their problems increased with great rapidity. One of the chief troubles was among the younger members of the crew, a rebelliousness which came close to open mutiny. To the captain the reason for it was beyond understanding.

"Three grandchildren for you and four for me does *not* constitute a population explosion!" Captain Deslann said hotly, the disagreement lines around Hellahar's mouth not helping his anger any. "Even if those numbers were doubled and all restraint removed from subsequent generations—and neither of those possibilities is likely to occur, first because your training methods come close to hypnoconditioning in their effects and secondly because of the fact that the incidence of male sterility is directly proportional to the degree of inbreeding—this is still a big ship and we can devote more compartments to food-growing. The problem is not immediate, but I can't make Haynor see that! The trouble with that young fool is that—"

"He's young?" said Hellahar quickly. "And we aren't?"

"I do not believe that my thought processes have atrophied to such an extent that—"

"Very often, sir," said Hellahar, "that is one of the symptoms."

112

Deslann kept silent for a long time. He was thinking that the healer had turned nasty in his old age, even though his mind had remained clear and sharp; and Deslann himself was not so old that he would suffer much more of such insubordination without doing something pretty drastic about it. When he went on his voice was quieter, more controlled, and much more angry.

He said, "Haynor has the highest intelligence and aptitude of anyone in his generation, which is one of the reasons for my anger and disappointment at him and his ridiculous ideas. If it wasn't for them I'd have no hesitation in naming him the next captain. But discounting the fact that he, as your son, will receive the benefit of any of your doubts, is there any sane reason for wasting reaction mass simply to come within visual distance of another ship?"

"Put like that, no sir," Hellahar replied, answering the question but ignoring the tone. "But this is not a completely sane situation we have here, and boredom is proportional to the level of intelligence and that is the main reason behind the support for Haynor's proposal. This is not my specialty, but if the idea could be modified and perhaps incorporated into the training program . . ."

It was grossly unnatural, Deslann knew as well as did the healer, for young, healthy, and intelligent people to have as their sole purpose in life the observation of colored lights and similar displays which always gave the same information, and hence required no corrective action, for year after year and sometimes for generation after generation. Despite the great stress placed on the importance and meaning of those lights there was a growing feeling, among some of the second generation trainees especially, that they were in fact only colored lights and to worry about them was silly. The flagship was their world and the things which the elders said were taking place outside it were very hard to believe. If another ship like their own, though, were to become clearly visible in one of the direct vision panels, Deslann told himself, that should take care of the doubts: It would furnish clear proof that each and every light in the winking vastness of the computer room was a ship and should be guided and cherished as such.

113

Unless the young fools began to doubt the evidence of their own eyes, or believed that the image in the direct vision panel was simply another display similar to the pictures shown on the educator screens . . .

Deslann began to feel angry again with Hellahar. The healer had an irritating habit of sending the captain's mind off at a tangent just when Deslann was on the point of figuratively tearing Hellahar's dorsal off and, what was even more irritating, the tangent usually ended in a question which just had to be answered and the process of finding the answer required all Deslann's attention so that the other's insubordination went not only unpunished but very often unremarked.

Despite the urgency of this problem Deslann was sure of one thing, he was *not* going to allow anyone to move the flagship. He had a brief, horrifying mental picture of the fleet arriving in the target system while its center of control was lost somewhere between the stars.

Yet, if the flagship were to remain in station it did not necessarily mean that one of the other ships could not be brought to them, one of the nearer expendables in the vanguard, for instance. The disadvantages were that his own trainee engineers would not get the chance to apply thrust to their own ship and the eager young astrogators and computer technicians would have to forego the pleasures of a massive reprograming which a shift in position of the control center would entail; on the other hand, the advantages were many—especially if Hellahar and himself were able to dramatize things so as to keep everyone interested for a long, long time.

Watching that single light signaling in the computer room its change of position as it slowly approached them—and it would be slow, because part of the drill would be on the control and guidance of ships over great distances using only the tiny reserve of reaction mass carried for predestination maneuvering—could be made something more than an interesting game. And when the expendable arrived—a brute of a ship a little more than one great Long Sleep tank filled with the largest domestic and food species left on Untha—the doubters would doubt no more, for the timers on the expendable ships were set to warm their cargo only on landing. If seeing the ship and being able to travel across to it was not enough, then having to chip a way through solid ice in search of more living space or a supply of meat should convince the most fanatical doubter of its reality.

There would be the more subtle and long-term effects as well. Another ship close by, even though it contained only cooled, nonintelligent domestic animals, would make space a much less lonely and frightening place, and it would be a constant reminder of the many other ships in the fleet and of their purpose. But like most projects of real importance on the ship, this one would take many years to complete.

Too many years, perhaps, for Deslann to see it through.

XVI

With the passing years the doctor's hair had gone white, Dickson's had gone gray, and the lieutenant commander's had gone completely. Both Jenny and Margaret had aged more than any of the men, but nobody mentioned this and there were no mirrors in *Gulf Trader* to tell them about it. The Game had become so much a part of their lives that it would have been harder to stop playing it than it would have been to stop breathing. With their children they made the great metal tanks echo to the songs of Bing Crosby and the tunes of Gilbert and Sullivan, or acted out famous plays or sometimes quite trivial incidents from their own past lives, or they had deep, philosophical discussions regarding the probable background, motivations, and future fictional actions of some very minor character in a remembered story (the doctor had completed a fourth story in the Hornblower series which, if C. S. Forester ever heard about it, would probably turn the poor man to cowboys and Indians).

They had a lot of fun when the discussion revolved around a minor character from one of Wallis's stories, a character who was not even human, but oddly enough it often happened that such humorous and ridiculous philosophizings became the most serious of them all. Even so, their lives were not all singing and sparkling conversation and fun. There was disaffection and quarreling and, at the times when Richard was directly involved, behavior which was close to mutiny.

At seventeen Richard had developed a positive genius for starting fights. One of his little exercises involved asking his seniors—the original survivors, that is, not his older brother or sister—for permission to engage in some activity which just might be allowable. He would ask their permission separately on this borderline matter, so that some were sure to give it while some would refuse, after which he would take his course of action much farther than his original request allowed, safe in the knowledge that he could play his seniors off against each other to such an extent that he would escape scot free. Many times Wallis had to stop arguments just short of violence by pulling rank, something he hated to do over such petty incidents. And more and more often he found himself telling Dickson and the doctor what he would like to do with Richard, from tying him neck deep in the bath for a couple of days to hanging him from the projecting outlet pipe in Number Four, which was the nearest thing they had to a yardarm.

Realizing that the commander was not even half joking when he said some of these things, the doctor took a special interest in Richard. The fact that they were the only bachelors on the ship gave them something in common, Radford said, and then he outlined his plan for giving them something else in common. When Wallis expressed his doubts regarding this proposal, the doctor went on to explain that Richard was at a difficult age and that the drives and pressures of adolescence were being aggravated by what must be admitted was a highly abnormal situation. It would probably help what ailed him if he was made to feel more important, or even superior in some ways to those around him. Most of Radford's specialized knowledge was too repetitious and boring for general distribution during the Game, but if he could interest Richard in becoming his successor . . .

Wallis still had doubts, but they disappeared five months later when the senior Dicksons and Wallises became grandparents twice over within a matter of minutes. It was a hectic time for everyone, especially for the doctor and Richard, who delivered two mothers of their babies practically simultaneously, but they coped very well with this emergency. When a measure of peace had returned to the tanks the seniors, who somehow had found themselves pushed out to the fringes of all the activity, did some serious talking about Richard.

"Your son is going to be a good doctor one of these days," Margaret Wallis told Jenny Dickson as they were

117

winding up the discussion. "You don't have to worry about him from now on. He'll settle down, you'll see."

"Of course he was simply following my lead," said the doctor smugly. "I admit that the second one arrived five minutes before I even saw it, but the fact still remains that—"

". . . He was following your lead," Dickson finished for him, and then added proudly, "from about twenty yards out in front!"

"A mere technicality," said the doctor. He looked even prouder of Richard than did his assistant's mother and father.

But Richard did not settle down to anything like the extent they expected of him, although as a person he became much less obnoxious—the doctor, thought Wallis, must have given him some intensive tuition in the bedside manner. He was plainly unhappy and discontented and kept putting forward ideas which were stupid or dangerous, or both. One of his more frequent proposals was for increasing the living space within the ship by opening a passage to the storage spaces under the bridge deck or to the aft pump room. In a weak moment Wallis gave him permission to go ahead on this project, because he was sure that the preparatory work would take such a long time that Richard would lose interest in it, but in this Wallis was wrong.

At that time the population of *Gulf Trader* was eleven, three of whom were very young children, and the doctor's garden covered two whole tanks. He had done this to absorb the extra wastes rather than because of a shortage of oxygen, and the air was so rich in this gas that he was advocating the burning of certain wastes to bring it down to a more normal level. When Richard asked if the garden would absorb carbon monoxide as well as the dioxide, the doctor said that he wasn't sure but he thought it would, and after that the ideas came thick and fast.

They would use the old generator's petrol engine and a compressor to refill the empty oxy and acetylene tanks with compressed air. As an extra precaution they would pipe the engine's exhaust into a tank of sea water in the garden, and the carbon monoxide which wasn't dissolved in the water would be absorbed by the plants. With compressed air available they would pierce the plating between themselves and a likely compartment, letting the water run out of it while replacing it with air. A lot of water would collect inside the ship, but there was no danger in this as they were fast aground and did not have to worry about buoyancy. When they had emptied the chosen compartment of water they would observe the rate at which it was refilled from outside leaks, if any, over a period of several "days" before cutting a way in. Provision would also be made for sealing the opening quickly in an emergency. And there were other ideas which could be developed as they went along . . .

By the time Richard had finished speaking, his brother, Joseph, and Wallis's son, David, were solidly behind him, and the lieutenant commander was beginning to wonder if his mind was not, perhaps, becoming a trifle inelastic in his old age, for he, also, was becoming caught up in Richard's enthusiasm although previously he had been dead against the project. But Wallis retained enough common sense to veto Richard's first choice of what he called the New Country to be opened.

Gulf Trader had gone aground bow first and had settled, since it lay on a shelving bottom, stern down. Richard's first plan was to drain the aft pump room. But the volume of water in the pump room was such that it would have flooded the three sternmost tanks to a depth of anything up to six feet, quite apart from the fact that it was almost certainly open to the sea. The second choice Wallis agreed with, after a long consultation with Dickson Senior.

It was a short length of corridor and two cabins which had been part of the stokers' living quarters, but which had been stripped to make room for some communications equipment due to come aboard at Liverpool. The corridor opened onto the weather deck via a watertight door and was interrupted by another such door six or seven yards later at a point for'rard of the companionways leading down to the engine room and up to the poop deck. When the second torpedo had struck aft there would have been direct access to the boat deck via the companionways for survivors from the engine room; the weather deck had

119

been awash, so nobody would have entered the corridor from that side; and the two cabins were no longer used by the crew. The chances, therefore, were very good that the watertight doors had not been opened, and the volume of water contained in the short stretch of corridor and the two cabins was not excessive.

The project took almost two years.

By way of a dress rehearsal Richard opened a way into the bilges through one of the modified intercostal spaces. There was an airtight hatch in the tank floor leading to the space, similar to the one used as a head, and another airtight cover on the floor of the tiny compartment underneath it which was not supposed to be opened until the ship was in drydock. Richard went into this compartment and had it sealed after him. He used his torch and compressed-air tank and sheer brute strength to open the lower hatch, and was able to look directly into the water-filled bilge while the extra air pressure kept the water from flooding up, and he could see fish swimming about. It was the first time he had seen a fish, or any living creature other than human beings, and the effect on him was something he would talk about for years. He replaced the lower hatch quickly before the light faded completely from his torch— its battery had been recharged so many times that it did not hold a charge for very long—and tapped to be let out.

They were not able to open the upper hatch slowly enough to avoid a sudden pressure drop, and Richard had an attack of nosebleed and trouble with his ears. But he was able to tell them that there was now a place to dump the growing pile of waste in Number One, as well as any other undesirable material.

Richard did not say it in so many words, but they all knew that there was now a place for their bodies to go when they died. . . .

Wallis thought about this useful if somewhat morbid discovery many times during the long wait for the stokers' cabins to drain, but he forgot it completely as the last of the water gurgled out of the new territory and he signaled for the opening to be made. If there should be a sudden deluge through the opening they would all get a soaking and have to abandon some useful material, but there

120

would be plenty of time to get out of Number Twelve and seal it behind them in an emergency. Besides, Wallis was as impatient now as was Richard to get up there, although unlike Richard he could not have stated his reasons with any clarity.

A few minutes later they were pushing their way through the opening, ignoring the scorched hands they received on the still-hot edges. Dickson Senior, Richard, the doctor, Eileen, and Wallis himself—everyone who was not either looking after the children or working the generator —ran laughing and shouting along the tiny stretch of corridor and in and out of the two cabins, stamping their feet like children in the pools of sea water still covering the deck and bumping into each other and talking hysterically about drying out the place and oiling the door hinges. But gradually they grew quiet and gathered silently around the two portholes.

In the port looking forward they could see the outline of the navigation deck and mainmast, dull shadows in a cool, green twilight, with the catwalk, weather deck rail, and derricks in much greater detail. The view over the side showed a sandy bottom with irregular outcroppings of reef. There were very few fish about and very little undersea plant life. Wallis had been surprised that the glass of the port had not been obscured by scum, and guessed that a strong current or tidal effect kept the greenery from taking hold. The view forward and upwards was cut off by the projecting poop deck, but the second port was set in the side of the ship.

It showed the towering, black precipice of a reef which soared upwards until it poked through the bright, dimpled mirror of the surface two hundred feet above them.

"Now," said the doctor, laughing suddenly, "I can tell the days and not just the months."

"Now," said Richard, in the most solemn voice that Wallis had ever heard him use, "I know that there is something outside the ship. . . ."

Shortly after that the joy and excitement of being able to see outside was damped suddenly. Up until then nobody on *Gulf Trader* had died.

Jenny was the first one to go. Richard knew every bit

121

as much as the doctor did about the treatment and control of diabetes, but there was no insulin on the ship and nothing that either of them could do. A little later Richard's father tripped and hit his head against a hatch coaming—his mind had not been on what he was doing, only on his dead Jenny—and he did not regain consciousness. Then Margaret caught what both the doctor and Richard agreed was pneumonia, and they broke the news as gently as possible to Wallis that there was nothing they could do for her, either, except to allow the lieutenant commander to stay in the sick bay with her for as long as possible. Wallis began the watch, which was both long and all too short, but he did not know exactly when she died. He had been holding her in his arms, with one eye closed and the other blinded with tears, for a long time when Richard tapped him gently on the shoulder and led him away.

After that the doctor and Wallis returned to sleeping together for warmth. But it was a very cold winter and for many months their age had made it impossible to exercise even briefly on the generator. More and more frequently Wallis lay shivering and sleepless, just as he had done when they were very recent survivors and worried about the possibility of escape and very little else. Now he was not worried, but the death of Margaret had left him with an aching sense of grief, which worsened with every passing day. It was as if he had lost a limb and the shock was beginning to wear off. But there were nights when he was able to sleep.

"What were you doing last night, sir?" the doctor said after one of them. They were at breakfast and he was obviously trying to cheer Wallis up. "When you grabbed me, for a minute I thought that you had designs on my virtue!"

"I'll sleep somewhere else," said Wallis.

The doctor was silent for a moment, then he said awkwardly, "I know how it was with you two. Putting your arm around me in your sleep doesn't bother me. I like it. To tell the truth—it doesn't make me feel so cold. I'm always cold these days. . . ."

A few days later Surgeon Lieutenant Radford made a self-

122

diagnosis of pneumonia and Wallis began another long, heartbreaking watch. This time it was shared by Richard, a young but strangely mature Richard who had grown close to the doctor over the past few years, as close as he had ever been to his parents. Richard watched dry-eyed and listened, in the doctor's increasingly brief lucid spells, to his mentor laying down the law.

"I've packed your head full of symptoms and diseases and treatments which you'll probably never get to use," Wallis heard him tell Richard on one occasion, "and as a result you are pretty good on theory. Your practical experience, on the other hand, is confined—if you'll excuse the pun—to maternity cases. You wouldn't know a liver or a transverse colon if they were to stand up and slap your face. You can't help that, of course, because we have no medical texts, or illustrations, or even the means of making decent sketches. But in a day or two you will be in a position to find out a few things and I urge you—no dammit, I *order* you!—to do so. You understand what I'm driving at? I do not want to go into the bilge all in one piece!"

Richard understood what the doctor was driving at, and so did Wallis.

"Good!" said Radford weakly. "We'll make a doctor out of you yet. But there's another thing—a small point, really, but it sort of makes your position official. I had to take it, and I'd the devil of a time remembering all of it. You can repeat it after me.

"I swear by Apollo the Physician, by Aesculapius, Hygeia, and Panacea, and I take to witness . . ."

Richard repeated the oath slowly and carefully, committing it to memory against the time when he might have to administer it to someone else. He was unlikely to forget it in any case, because people on the ship did not forget things, the Game saw to that. But it was a long time before Richard would answer to his title without looking uncomfortable or objecting to its use.

And then the time came when Wallis himself began to display the old familiar symptoms—rendered unfamiliar only because he was viewing them from the inside—of shivering, of coughing fit to tear his chest apart, and of increasing periods of delirium. He could not die well like Doctor Radford; he was so afraid that he rarely spoke at all. In his later lucid periods, though, he lay thinking about the sky and trees and Margaret, and worrying about the hole they had all made in the ship's food supply. There would be no actual shortage for a long, long time, but David or Joseph should begin thinking seriously about growing food to augment the canned supply. And he lay listening to his children and the Dickson's and all their grandchildren playing the Game.

It was a story he had always liked, about a civilization that had grown up in a giant interstellar ship lost forever among the stars, with Joseph taking the part of Hugh Hoyland and his son that of the mutant Joe-Jim. But they made it a short story. Wallis overheard Richard telling everyone there would not be time enough to recite the dying Commander's favorite novel. Considering the situation in *Gulf Trader,* Wallis thought, it was a rather appropriate story.

XVII

Deslann was succeeded by Haynor, who was succeeded by his son of the same name, who was succeeded by Helltag the Mad, who was killed by the third Haynor. The population of the Unthan flagship had stabilized at forty to fifty people, the larger proportion of which were female. This was a troublesome situation, both potential and actual, but a minor one compared with the terrible problem of inbreeding. A significant increase in the incidence of male sterility had been expected and planned for, also certain physical deformities and weakening of the intellect. They did not expect the large-headed throwbacks to presapient times, who had to be restrained long before they reached maturity because of their predatory habits, nor did they foresee the birth of outwardly normal offspring whose minds grew more monstrous and twisted than the bodies of their unfortunate brothers and who were still intelligent enough to conceal their mental abnormalities as had Captain Helltag.

The third Haynor was not above average in physical or mental ability and he was not even a trainee captain —of the five young engineering pupils in training at that time, he rated number four. But he was on watch in the control room with his engineer tutor when Captain Helltag, in a perfectly normal tone of voice, said, "Nothing ever happens in this place," and unlocked the Fleet Landing Board. Before the other two realized what he was doing, more than thirty units of the fleet—the main fleet, that is, not just the food vessels in the vanguard—had been given random changes of attitude thrust of random duration applied through their main drives.

Shouting at Helltag about the hundreds of cold-sleeping colonists in each of those misdirected ships, the engineer darted towards the captain to restrain him by force, since it was obvious now that Helltag was no longer rational. But Haynor's tutor was much older than Helltag and his attempt to knock the captain away from the control board only made the other turn vicious as well as irrational. A sudden dark fog grew around the old officer's body. Helltag was using his teeth. . . .

Haynor joined the struggle then, trying to get a hold on Helltag behind the dorsal and baring his own teeth. One of the trainee healers had told him about a weak spot which, when firmly pressed by the teeth or other small, firm object, caused temporary paralysis and loss of consciousness. Haynor found the spot all right, but just as he was applying pressure to it Helltag twisted toward him suddenly and Haynor's teeth punctured the captain's skin and tore the area deeply.

Helltag went violently out of control then, tried to tie his body into a physically impossible knot, and died.

Because he was a trainee engineer, and not a very promising one at that, Haynor had very little knowledge or appreciation of the tremendous amount of responsibility devolving upon the flagship's commander. But he had stopped Helltag from killing the aging engineer and from wreaking even greater havoc among the fleet. After all, the safety of their thousands of cold-sleeping charges—the last survivors of Untha's past and the only hope of her future—was something taught early and often, so that Haynor found himself promoted to captain for reasons which were purely emotional. Despite this Haynor made a very good captain. During his reign he was able to inspire the astrogation and computer departments into correcting the courses of the ships Helltag had sent astray —a job requiring close to two decades of time and an order of fine computation of which the great Gerrol himself would have been proud.

The appointment of Haynor, however, good in itself as everyone agreed at the time, set dangerous precedents: The precedent of promotion across the lines of specialty and training. Promotion based on psychological factors of an emotional and personal nature rather than on technical ability. And the solution of problems, or the resolution of difficult situations, by physical violence.

126

For the flagship civil war was not many generations away.

From the sweating bulkheads of Number One to the Commander's Ladder in Twelve, and from Richard's Hole in the bilges to Richard's Rooms under the poop deck, a philosophical war was brewing. On one side were the old people and the majority of the women, all of whom believed that the material handed down through the years by way of the Game was fact, solid, immutable fact containing precisely the same degree of reality as, say, the recollection of the first stumbling words of one's own child only a few years away in time. Some of these people were so fanatical in their beliefs that there were times when they confused remembered fiction with remembered fact. But the other side went to the opposite extreme, being fanatically cynical about practically everything. Somewhere in the middle was Dr. Kimball Bush Dickson.

It was his professional duty to be neutral, of course, but his neutrality was further assured by the fact that in matters outside his profession he was very easily swayed.

At the present time, however, the doctor was alone and his opinions were all his own. Striding briskly through the absolute darkness of the midships tanks on his way to Richard's Rooms, he thought they would all have been better advised to worry about the increasing corrosion and dampness in the tanks, the mounting number of mechanical and electrical failures, and the diminishing supply of canned food, light bulbs, and material suitable for clothing. But to be perfectly fair, the doctor knew that they did worry, especially the younger people, and very often they tried to do something about these problems. The trouble was that they tended to be a little cynical about the effects of external water pressure and the behavior of electric current, which meant that there were periodic power failures and that in winter the air was so damp that it was difficult to keep warm even following a turn on one of the generators, and so the incidence of death from respiratory diseases in the very young and old was increasing as well. Maybe if they *all* listened a little more carefully to each other and worked together on these problems something could be done. Again, maybe not.

He was at a loss to understand the reason for the split in the first place. It was nothing so simple as impetuous youth fighting senile decay. Because of the necessity for conserving food, water, and to a lesser extent air, there was nothing to do all day except exercise one's brain, so that physical methods of self-expression were discouraged by young and old alike. Fighting among themselves, a closed community in such a harsh environment, was unthinkable. And while the youths might be mentally impetuous the oldsters were not mentally senile. On *Gulf Trader* there was no such condition.

His hereditary medical knowledge, the doctor had good reason to believe, had reached him subject to less change over the years than some material he could think of—the discipline of his specialized, traditionally unmarried predecessors had been strict. Doctor Radford, the First, had stated that their hair and teeth might fall out, but the Game had trained their minds to such a fine pitch that they need never fear becoming dotards.

The doctor walked across the floor of Number Twelve and began climbing the ladder, still without putting a hand or a foot wrong. It was not until he ascended to Richard's Rooms and the absolute darkness gave way to the dim, bluish light from the portholes that he began to trip and stumble, and that was because he was using his eyes to judge distances instead of relying on memory to tell him the exact positions of things. Greeting the five young people who were sitting cross-legged around the cabin, he picked his way between them to stand at the port. While the others resumed talking he looked out and up through the scummy glass.

The outlines of the navigation bridge and deck fittings and the towering precipice of the reef on the port side had an intensity of blackness almost frightening, as if the gray light filtering down from the surface was being absorbed hungrily and sucked away into some other continuum, never to escape again as a highlight or reflection. When an occasional phosphorescent creature blew past in

128

the current it seemed almost dazzling against those inky shadows.

It was a moonlit night up there, with little if any cloud. Clouds were shapeless collections of water vapor at a great height which could totally obscure the Moon but could not do the same with the light of the Sun, and which under certain conditions released water over a large area—but slowly, as if a ceiling had sprung hundreds of tiny leaks. The Moon was an arid, airless body of near-planetary dimensions circling the Earth at a distance of approximately 238,000 miles and shone by the reflected light of the Sun, a G-type star situated near the rim of the parent galaxy. . . .

Or so the older people would have said. And if asked—or even if they had not been asked—they would have added a mind-staggering weight of astronomical detail. But the younger people sitting around him, especially the thirteen-year-old Arthur Sullivan Wallis, might have said that the people on the surface were operating their standby generator while checking the wiring of the big one, just as they did on the ship. The doctor knew that the people for'rard believed in their G-type sun, but that ASW did not wholly believe in his stupendous topside generator which probably needed thousands of people to work its pedals. Arthur Sullivan Wallis did not wholly believe in anything.

At the moment, however, there was nothing wild or heretical about the things he was saying. The doctor turned from the porthole to listen.

". . . So the food can't last forever even if we agree to drastically reduce the future population," Arthur was saying. "*Everybody* agrees to this measure, particularly when they have just become parents for the first time and realize what a dangerous and painful thing childbirth is in this place. But usually it isn't until the second time that they do anything about it. In any case the population is going down due to worsening living conditions. It hasn't been as low as twelve since—"

"We could grow more food," said his sister, Irene Mac-Dougall Wallis.

"That would help with the clothing problem, too," said

129

her cousin, Bing Churchill Dickson. "Plant fiber material can't be made into an overall, it comes apart too easily and it can't be washed at all. But it's warm and if we had more growing plants—"

"I agree," said Randolph Brutus Dickson, the fourth member of the group. "Even though shredded beanstalks itch like blazes, I prefer them to going around raw like this. I haven't felt warm since I was a baby."

The fifth member of the party laughed. She was Elizabeth Graves Wallis and she laughed at everything. When she wasn't laughing she smiled silently and played with her fingers, and she was without doubt the happiest person in the ship.

"Extending the garden won't work," Arthur resumed patiently, "because we haven't the necessary wiring or light bulbs. At the rate we're blowing them they won't outlast the food supply, and increasing the number of lighting points will use them up that much quicker. No bulbs means no light, no beans, and no air. As I see it there is no solution to the problem within the ship, which means that we must work towards rescue."

At that point the doctor began to feel a little bit disappointed in ASW. Methods of attracting the attention of the people on the surface were always being tried, although much less frequently of late, from simple banging on the hull in Morse to running lights into Richard's Rooms and flashing them through the portholes at night. But the attempts had served only to make everyone unhappy for months afterwards, and now they were actively discouraged. Thinking about rescue was like thinking about girls, a phase of youth.

"My idea was to use the Rooms here," Arthur went on, "to get one of us to the surface. The door to the weather deck is rusted solid and the same goes for the portholes, but I was thinking of smashing the glass and squeezing through, or being pushed through by an adult, and swimming to the surface. To get through the port it would have to be a seven- or eight-year-old. Or ten, maybe, if he was thin enough.

"He would have to be well briefed on what to say to the people up there," ASW went on, "and would carry something—a message and the lieutenant commander's identity card, perhaps—so that if he didn't make it to the shore alive, or his verbal report was not believed at first, they would still know we were here. . . ."

"J-just a minute!" the doctor broke in aghast. "You can't do that! The port would be a tight squeeze even for a skinny eight-year-old, and there would be jagged edges of glass around the rim. You couldn't be sure of breaking all of them away with the water pouring in. The kid would be cut to ribbons on the way out!"

"The adult," said Arthur seriously, "would be a volunteer who knew that he was going to die, so he would not panic. He would be tied in position so that the inrush of water would not sweep him away from the port, and while the boy kept his head in the air for as long as possible and hyperventilated, the adult would knock all of the loose glass from the rim of the port. When the water rose above the top edge of the port the air trapped in the upper part of the room would slow the influx of water and allow plenty of time for the boy to be assisted through the port—"

"No!"

This time it was Irene who objected, and she sounded personally afraid rather than shocked at the idea as she went on, "It would mean losing the Rooms and making the ship *blind*! I don't think I could stand that. Our parents might—they don't like coming here because they can see out and that makes them uncomfortable. But I want to know that there is somewhere else besides the ship, something else besides rusting metal walls and damp bedding and this everlasting cold and stench.

"I'd like to live up here," she added vehemently, "and look out at the light all the time. No matter what it is that makes it."

There was a long silence, broken by Arthur who said, "I agree with you completely, Irene. That's why I mentioned my second-best idea first. The other one involves no children, but we would have to use Richard's Hole for purposes other than the one for which it was intended. . . ."

The doctor listened without interrupting while Arthur Sullivan Wallis expanded on his best idea, thinking that a person less timid than himself would have been laying down the law in no uncertain terms after the first few sentences. Even so, when he did finally speak, Dr. Kimball Bush Dickson thought that his voice carried a little of the rasp possessed by the first doctor when someone was being wilfully stupid.

He said, "The bilges are impassable, Arthur, you *know* that! We've been told that people have died cleaning out the bilges on ships like this: They lost their way among the intercostal spaces and couldn't find the way back to the entry point. Even with lights and the bilge water only a few inches deep it would be next to impossible to travel half the length of the ship through the space between the double bottom—it's too tight a squeeze, for one thing. In pitch darkness with the bilges completely under water and dragging an air hose and trying to hold your helmet vertical all the time—!"

"I'll be careful with the hose," said Arthur, in a voice which must have been identical to that used by his ancestor Richard when his seniors were trying to argue him out of opening up the Rooms, "and the helmet will be tied to my shoulders. The idea is to use a bucket filled with air fed through the hose from the hole. It will be open at the bottom so that I'll have to keep my head upright to keep the air from spilling out, and there will be no need of a visor because it will be dark anyway.

"I've thought about this for a long time," he went on seriously, "and have decided to try for the stern opening. The torpedo which hit the bow opened the forepeak, and to reach there would mean climbing up through the forward coffer dam, which is thought to be badly damaged and perhaps blocked with wreckage. The second torpedo struck below the waterline astern, and its opening is much closer to the Hole—"

"You've thought about it," the doctor broke in, "but not enough, obviously! Did you think about the scavengers we see in the Hole? They're all *small* fish, not more than two inches across. If nothing bigger can get in how are you going to get out?"

Arthur's teeth glowed briefly in the dark as he smiled. "Maybe the bigger fish aren't interested in getting in, Doc-

132

tor, when there are so many small fish more easily got at outside."

"Doesn't it bother you," said the doctor, trying another tack, "that during the first dozen yards of your journey you will be crawling through the bones of all the people who have died in the ship? Some of them have died quite recently and the scavengers might not have finished with them . . ."

"Now," said Arthur scornfully, "you're beginning to sound like my father recalling an Edgar Allan Poe—"

The doctor kept on arguing, off and on, until the day early in the following spring when Arthur Wallis and Randy Dickson, who was to see to the paying out of the hose, made the escape attempt, even though he had realized long since that he was simply wasting his breath.

The long, narrow, rusting world of *Gulf Trader* lay cold and dark and silent. With both its generators still and the women moved far forward into One with orders to keep the children quiet at all costs, the only sounds in the ship were made by Arthur's bucket helmet scraping the other side of the deck beneath their feet. Barefoot, shivering, and speaking in whispers if they spoke at all, they traced Arthur's slow progress from Richard's Hole to the inter-costals under Eleven. At that point he was more than halfway to the holed stern, with just the spaces under Twelve, the aft coffer dam, the fuel bunker, and the more confined spaces under the engine-room flat still to go. But it was at that point that something went wrong.

The scraping of Arthur's helmet against the metal floor became louder and more erratic, and there was a softer, muffled sound as if he might have been banging on the plating with his fists. Shortly afterwards the noises stopped.

XVIII

Somebody had committed the unforgivable crime of moving a packing case without previously notifying the change of position. The case could very well have been moved accidentally by one of the children playing, although none of them would admit to doing so, and the change of position was less than two yards. But Irene Mac-Dougall Wallis walked into it in the dark and painfully bruised her knee and thigh. The pain and the fright and the recent death of her brother Arthur under Tank Eleven all contributed to what happened then.

The split began because of Irene's insistence that the case had been moved deliberately, with malice aforethought, and that its movement constituted an act of violence on someone's part, and she further insisted that the someone in question could only be one or more of the seniors. Until then the history of the ship had been free from violence—the small domestic rows did not count, being purely verbal affairs—so that the incident of the packing case caused a lot of bad feeling. Despite the efforts of the doctor the rift could not be closed, and gradually the young people moved their living quarters aft. They started their own garden in Eleven, and they organized their own Game.

They took their turn on the generator and occasionally, when the Seniors wanted to dig out an operetta or a Shakespeare, they would send a couple of good voices to complete the cast. There was very little said, however, during generator duty and the exchanges of talent became fewer. Inevitably the Young People grew old themselves and had difficult, rebellious young people of their own to contend with, but the common ground of parenthood was not enough to close the widening rift between the two factions. All the knowledge of the original survivors to-

134

gether with the intervening ship history was available to both groups by way of the Game, but now history was beginning to diverge.

There were no further acts of violence, however, although the deaths directly attributable to the split grew at an alarming rate—at least the doctors, who traditionally had a foot in each camp, found them so. The stern section was the coldest part of the ship and damp and corrosion had taken the strongest hold there. Infant mortality was high and the adults rarely lived beyond the mid-fifties. And in each generation there was at least one young, intelligent, and relatively healthy boy or girl who died, like Arthur Sullivan Wallis, in the frigid darkness of the bilges trying to escape from the only world they knew.

And far, far above them other men and women were escaping from their world, to places like the Moon and Mars and the Jovian satellites. Some of them died, too.

The third and final expedition against the food ship led by Captain Deslann the Fifth hung like a slow-moving shoal of fish between the flagship and the target vessel. Unlike the tiny creatures which their ancestors had known on Untha, these fish had to carry a little of their ocean with them, and there was barely enough of it to take them to the enemy ship. That was one of the reasons why peace talks were at the moment still going on between the enemy captain and his senior communications officer—so Deslann Five thought cynically as the two voices sounded in his suit communicator. His enemy counterpart was old and short-tempered and male like himself while the comm officer was very young and female and unusually well gifted with intelligence and self-assurance, so that the combination was unlikely to produce a peaceful settlement to their problem. It might, however, cause enough of a diversion in the enemy ship to allow the expedition to land undetected.

Deslann Five had to remind himself firmly that he was on the side of Right, otherwise his feelings of shame would have reached uncomfortable proportions.

"Asking about the health of our children," Captain

Hellseggorn in the food ship was saying angrily, "is merely a preliminary to inquiring about the number of them, which is a transparent attempt to discover the probable strength of the present adult population. Do you think we are stupid? The children are doing well—they get enough meat, you see—and the number of adults, while less than yours, since over here we don't proliferate like wild rulties, is sufficient. We are not going back to the flagship, and if you try forcing us to do so you will find it as effective as your present stupid arguments!

"Why don't you simply ask for food, which is what you really want?" Hellseggorn went on. "The answer will still be 'No,' of course, because you wouldn't stop at taking food. Our ancestors escaped your brand of fanaticism six generations ago, and I will not allow any of my people to be reconverted to that . . . that . . ."

"The discipline isn't nearly so strict now," the quiet, feminine, maddeningly reasonable voice from the flagship broke in. "We no longer insist on six or more trainees for every post, and the captain's position, which is the most important, has only two understudies. And we realize, sir, that it was the too-rigid insistence on purely technical training which drove your forebears into living on the food ship. We did not expect them to cut down on the supply of meat, which aggravated the situation. Especially as your ship is so packed with food animals that you could never eat your way through them in a hundred generations. But now there is ample opportunity for cultural as well as technical studies, so that you no longer have anything to fear in that respect."

If he had not had this ridiculous feeling of shame over what they were doing, the captain would have admired the smooth manner in which the young female was moving from a criticism of Hellseggorn's ancestors and her own to a criticism of Hellseggorn himself. The water in the food ship's control room had been heated, by now it must be coming close to the boil.

"You are intelligent enough without doubt," she went on, in a tone which was pleasant but just a shade doubtful, "to realize that we can bring another food ship to ourselves if the situation warrants it, and ignore you. But we did not wish to ignore you or to waste another ship whose animals are needed to populate the seas of the target world with a food supply which we can be sure will suit our metabolism. We want you to be reunited with us, and soon.

"We are approaching the target sun."

There was a moment's silence, then Hellseggorn said furiously, "We have been approaching the target sun since the moment of take-off, and all these arguments have been used, with very few variations, on my parents and grandparents, and they have invariably ended with the climactic piece of data that the target sun was practically warming up our nose cones—a piece of data at which, apparently, we were expected to tie ourselves in knots and blow green bubbles from sheer ecstasy. All it did then, and does now, is make us angrier! Lying is bad enough, but a lie as unoriginal as that is an insult to the intelligence!

"I am breaking contact—"

"No, wait!" said the flagship urgently. "This is all true, sir! You know that your ship was meant to be a sub-fleet leader with a crew of three but was later changed to an unmanned slave under the control of the flagship. Your control room has manual overrides for certain internal controls—lighting, warming, and jettisoning the cargo—which had to be tested during the final stages of construction. But you have no control of your main drive, neither have you any means of seeing outside your ship—"

"We can't see," Hellseggorn shouted, "so if you tell us space is bright pink with yellow stars we must believe you!" He added a remark very rarely made by a male Unthan toward a female of the species, dealing as it did with certain abnormal methods of reproduction.

"Personally I don't care if you believe me or not!" the comm officer shouted back. She was really angry now, and not just baiting him. "We *are* getting close to the target sun! We are *not* interested in you solely because of your food supply, although meat would certainly improve our health. Our main concern is for your children. . . ."

Deslann Five thudded gently into the vast wall that was the food ship's side, and wriggled until all his padded magnets were in contact with the plating. By that time the rest of his party, all twenty-eight of them, had also arrived

137

and secured themselves. As quickly as possible they moved to the midships lock, a personnel lock used when the ship had been abuilding in orbit around Untha, and began opening its outer seal. What they were doing might very well be registering on the control-room telltales, but they hoped nobody was looking at them. Their water was beginning to taste stale.

". . . Our healers feel strongly about this," the angry female voice was saying, "and so do I! It's an unnatural life for any child, or an adult for that matter. The low temperature, for one thing, must have an inhibiting effect on their intelligence—this is a known and accepted fact, our healers say. And with all respect, sir, since you had no control over your childhood environment, I suggest that your own inability to grasp . . ."

The water in the food ship's control room exploded into steam at that point, metaphorically speaking, as Hellseggorn reacted to the suggestion that he was mentally retarded. Deslann and his party were packed into the lock, outer seal closed and inner seal open, directing as many cutting beams as could be brought to bear on the ice on the other side. In their case the explosions of steam, mixed with hot water and chunks of melting ice, made the metaphor almost literally true.

Deslann Five stayed in the lock while the others went to extend their bridgehead. He was trying to find the connection to the lock's outside antenna so as to reestablish contact with the flagship, lost when they had penetrated the metal hull of the food ship. When he discovered it and plugged it in, he found his communications officer speaking on another wavelength.

". . . Can you hear me, sir?" the female was saying worriedly. "They know something is going on. I repeat, they are sure that it is an attack but are not yet certain of the exact locality. Flagship to Captain Deslann. The food ship has now broken contact, but they know something is going on."

"Got it," said Deslann. "You did very well, Hayellin. Stay on that wavelength, it's clearer . . ."

Suddenly Deslann could not breathe. The water in his suit was like thick, warm mud and his vision was going.

138

Desperately he tore off the plates of his suit covering his gills and wriggled furiously to expel the foul water, but the fresh water which came in was so hot that he grunted in agony. On the point of losing consciousness he grabbed two pieces of ice which were hanging nearby and pressed them against his gills. When he breathed slowly the water passing around the ice was cooled enough not to scald his lungs. Then as soon as he could speak again he detailed one of his party to stand by the communicator and swam quickly through the inner seal.

Inside the lock a large hemisphere had been melted out of the solid ice filling the main hold of the food ship, a hemisphere which looked tiny only because the hold was so vast. It was expanding slowly as his party attacked the icy walls with their heat beams and it was filled with water close to boiling in some places while a short distance further on the water was icy cold. And there were chunks of ice, some of them as big as Deslann, which hung like invisible rocks in his path. The rear half of one of the food animals filling the hold, a thick, torpedo shape ending in a broad, razor-edged tail, projected from the ice wall on one side, and the head and dorsal of another animal from the other. The expression on its face, frozen there when it and its companions in the hold had been cooled so many generations ago, made Deslann want suddenly to laugh.

With all the movement inside the hemisphere, the temperature of the water would find a more comfortable level and the blocks of ice would shrink, but the food animals might not survive their partial warm-up—they were tough, but their revival required a sudden rise in temperature together with a carefully timed dose of the radiation which would shock their hearts and nervous systems back into life. But it was not, Deslann told himself, as if these two would be the only beasts rendered permanently rather than temporarily dead.

Peering through the ice at the twisted, frozen bodies he could see several whose edible parts were missing. The partly eaten bodies were grouped together and were surrounded by a pinkish fog, and a narrow band of fog ran through the center of the hold towards the bow. He knew

139

from intelligence gathered by the second expedition that the enemy did not have heat beams but, in melting their tunnels, used chemical methods which left a pinkish residue on the ice walls. Deslann gave orders quickly, and with their gill openings packed with chips of ice they began melting their way through to the enemy tunnel.

And in the tunnel they found the water suddenly blackened with mud bombs and out of the murk there came darting a stream of silvery, metal fish. The fish moved fairly slowly since they were being fired from spring-loaded guns at extreme range, but when they met their target, no matter how gently, a charge at the rear of the dart exploded driving the barb deeply into the fabric of the spacesuits and the flesh beneath. Deslann, who was in the lead, blundered into a chunk of ice and began pushing it ahead of him as a shield, but the people following him were not so lucky. A lot of the metal darts were slipping past his shield and the tunnel throbbed with the coughs and grunts of the wounded and with the pounding of their suddenly uncontrollable bodies against the walls and each other as the coating on the metal barbs attacked their nervous systems.

But the blackness around him was beginning to lighten, and the tunnel was opening out into the main living pool. Suddenly the enemy, males, females, and children, were all around them, easy targets for their own dart guns despite the nursery nets and decorative vegetation scattered about the pool. Their darts had been treated by the flagship's healers with a fast-acting anaesthetic—they were not, after all, on a mission of extermination—and the enemy did not have the protection of spacesuits. But the food-ship people did not know that the darts striking them were nonlethal and fought bitterly with guns, lances, and even teeth. The numbers of dead and dying on both sides continued to rise steadily, because Deslann's people had taken too much punishment and were killing mad. Instead of anaesthetic darts they were beginning to use their heat beams.

"If you have to kill them," the captain shouted urgently, "kill females!"

Then finally it was all over. The control room and associated compartments, the secondary pools and their connecting tunnels were searched and cleared of all sentient Unthan life. The dead were left to drift in water that was already cooling into the ice which would hold them immobile like the other beasts thronging the ship. The survivors, who were mainly children, had been moved to the flagship and only Deslann Five and the enemy captain were left.

"We were telling you the truth," Deslann said angrily as he, too, left the food ship, pushing the spacesuited and badly injured body of Captain Hellseggorn before him. "Although we could not risk telling you all of it, your minds back there were closed, you were no longer completely civilized, and we did not know how you might react. But we did not want your meat supply alone, and we did desperately want to be reunited with you.

"Surely you must have noticed," he went on, "that the expedition, with the exception of myself, was made up entirely of females. The reason for that is because the number of males born to us on the flagship has fallen to one in twenty, and the majority of those have been sterile.

"So we needed you, badly," Deslann the Fifth went on furiously, "and we did not want you dead. We were not intending to kill any of you, except by accident, and we were relying on surprise. From the previous expedition we learned that your children, unlike ours, were healthy and more evenly balanced as to sex. We think your diet had something to do with that. But we badly need those children.

"Without them there would be no future, no crew to man the flagship and guide the fleet during the most important stage of the journey. Surely you see that."

But Captain Hellseggorn was not seeing anything. During the last few minutes of the fighting he had swum through a patch of water freshly boiled by a heat beam and his eyes, like the mind behind them, were permanently closed in blindness. He could not see the two great ships which hung in the darkness ahead of and behind him, or the single star which blazed like a beacon against a backdrop of fainter suns. He could not see and would not believe that the journey's end was so very, very near.

XIX

In the stern section of *Gulf Trader* the settlement
of the Young People did not prosper well after the
third generation. First there was the serious blow to their
morale caused by the ports in Richard's Rooms becoming
covered with a thin green scum which rendered them
translucent rather than transparent and finally completely
opaque. They could no longer look out at the sandy sea bed
or the rocks or at the wrinkled, silvery surface far above
them, so that all these things became secondhand facts, or
part of the Game, and took the first step toward becoming
fiction. The second major misfortune was that the three
young couples were suffering, as was everyone else in
the ship, from vitamin deficiencies affecting their hair among
other things. The men were prematurely bald and two of
the women's hair had gone gray in patches and was
falling out. But the worst misfortune, a medical disaster in
the doctor's opinion, was that the female Young People
were all expecting babies.

In the ordinary way a child born into the world of the
ship could expect to receive hair both from its mother's
head and its father's head and chin. The early uniforms
and sacking had long since been worn to tatters and even
the tatters had rotted away in the increasingly damp atmosphere, so that clothing made from human hair was all
that an infant had to keep it warm between birth and the
age when it gained enough intelligence and physical control
to wear the stiffer vegetable fibers. Plant fibers were useful
for bedding and little else, and even the clothing made from
a mixture of plant and hair came apart or wore out too
easily. Hair was warm, flexible, and easily worked, and its
only disadvantage was that it took so long to grow.

For many generations it had been the custom to cut
hair off at the roots, regardless of age or sex, as soon as

142

it reached a useful length. The only exceptions were in the cases of young people close to maturity, who were allowed to retain their hair since they could be expected to marry within a few years and would want their first-born to be warmly clothed.

A male beard, no matter how bushy or luxuriant, could supply only a small fraction of the quantity grown on a healthy head. But the hair of the Young People couples, not to mention their general health, left much to be desired in the doctor's opinion, and this deficiency caused such deep concern among them that their Game suffered and for days at a stretch almost died from the psychological poison of worry. That was one of the reasons why the doctor offered to help out by donating his own sparse growth when next it became due for cutting.

Dr. James Eichlan Wallis was nineteen years old and suffered from a badly twisted spine (his mother, an epileptic, had had several falls during the later stages of her pregnancy) and a visually and tactually repulsive skin condition. His offer, as he knew it would be, despite his many reassurances that the condition was not transmissible, allowed him to take advantage of their resulting feelings of awkwardness over the refusal: by pressing his arguments for having them forget their senseless, and by now almost nonexistent, differences with the Seniors for'rard.

Except for the very infrequent visits of the elected commander aft for the purpose of marriage and the five-yearly inspection and the times when the Young People went amidships to serve in absolute silence on the generator, the only contact between the two groups was the doctor. He was able to tell them, therefore, of the greater comfort of the Senior living quarters, of the extra warmth and of the reserves of clothing available in an emergency—which could make all the difference to a patient in shock. He admitted that the improvement in conditions would be fractional, but important nonetheless, and at times his arguments were so vehement that for days on end the Young People refused to talk to him. Even the Seniors displayed toward him a certain coolness due to some of his arguments which had been loud enough to carry the length of the ship, and to the things he had said which were not intended to be heard by both sides. The one argument he could not use, partly because he was the doctor and partly because the change in living quarters was unlikely to affect the result, was to tell the Young People females the truth about their chances of surviving their approaching confinements.

He was disappointed, but not surprised, when his arguments got him precisely nowhere.

Until . . .

The first girl died in childbirth, not surprisingly considering her history of repeated bouts of rheumatic fever as a child and the condition in which it had left her heart. Her baby, a girl, gave a satisfactory cry on being smacked, but a few seconds later became cyanosed and died. A few days later the father died from a fractured skull sustained when he fell from Richard's Rooms to the floor of Number Twelve. He had somehow managed to avoid the ladder on his way down, and the indications were that he had not put his arms out to help break his fall.

Two Senior women arrived bringing a rusty tin of powdered milk, nearly two pounds of hair, and unlimited amounts of sympathy and help. Their action in coming aft was tantamount to mutiny, but they explained that they could not bear to listen to the harrowing details of life in the Young People's section which the doctor kept giving them. And so, despite a history in all respects the same as her predecessor, the second mother managed to cling to life, and so did her baby son. The third girl, whose physical condition was the worst of all, did not survive, although her daughter did. Coincidentally, the baby's father had an accident on the generator a few days later—a real rather than a deliberate accident, this time.

The gearing had jammed just as he had worked up to full speed and he was pressing down hard on the left pedal. Foot pressure snapped the pedal in half and the raw edge tore an eight-inch gash in his leg. The doctor sutured with hair and bound it tightly with leaves and plant fiber, which was the best he could do, but the man was a bleeder and there was never any hope for him.

It was at this point that the Young People became reabsorbed into the Seniors. At first there was a certain awkwardness—a feeling that the Seniors were simply performing a duty toward the surviving Young People, much as a family will look after the newly orphaned children of a distant and not very well-liked relative—but gradually this awkwardness disappeared. The newcomers were eagerly absorbing material which had been allowed to drop from the Young People's Game and in turn they were bringing three generations of fresh, new memories to the Seniors' Game. Some of this data included dialogue on the planning, preparation, and execution of four separate escape attempts, and they were without doubt the most stirring passages in the whole history of the submerged ship. It was as if some heavy, invisible load had been lifted from them by the simple fact of their being reunited. The whole, as the trite old saying had it, really was greater than the sum of its parts.

The deck and wall plating of all the tanks were red and gritty with rust, except for one wall of the generator room which was kept clean and smooth for purposes of education. In the condensation which formed there every day was written the alphabet or passages from books, or pictures or characters out of stories, or completely original compositions of words or pictures. And the Game itself was taking on a new and original dimension. As well as operetta, plays, stories, and sections of ship history being sung and acted out there was the exciting exploratory work being done on the probable background and motivation of subsidiary characters, particularly villains and extraterrestrials whose characterization always had been unsatisfactory from the point of view of credibility and depth. Some of this work was the most amusing, stimulating, and downright rewarding that had ever been done on the ship. Still, the renaissance did not stop short at the purely intellectual and artistic exercises of the Game.

During the months of summer they spent a few minutes each day hammering out an SOS on the hull. They felt a little ridiculous doing this, but in some obscure fashion it strengthened their faith in a world outside themselves and their ship. The insulation of their wiring kept rotting and peeling away, causing shorts and blowing out bulbs that were in terribly short supply, and leaving the ship without light for days on end. An ambitious project for rewiring the tanks and rebuilding the generator was initiated and carried through to a successful conclusion. Only three of the tanks were being lit while two sections of the garden were allowed to die in darkness, for so much of the wiring had to be discarded as useless; however, there were nowhere near as many people as there had been in the old days and fewer lighting points meant fewer bulbs wasted.

Another daring attempt, based on the facts that glass is a good conductor of heat and that plant life tends to wither and die when subject to a sudden rise in temperature, gave the ship back its sight: There had been a real danger of cracking the porthole glass and flooding Richard's Rooms and the whole of Number Twelve below them if heat from a fire had been applied too quickly; but instead the green scum that had gathered on the outside of the ports had turned yellow and peeled away. If they were willing to brave the cold and damp of the Rooms, and many of them were, they'd be able to look out at the rocks and sandy bottom and up at the restless, wrinkled sky or watch inquisitive fish watching them. . . .

They even ran a light to the Rooms, using the best of the discarded wiring and being especially careful to protect the circuit with fuses so that the precious light bulbs would not suffer. The light was to be used only in an emergency, for signaling purposes.

The rust was everywhere and it abraded his bare feet as he walked, but the doctor could remember it no other way, and the seams of the tank plating sweated constantly as the water outside tried to push its way through. That also was normal, although it was said that in the good old days the tank walls were clean and bone dry. The tanks themselves were supposed to have been filled with bright, clean tools and equipment, their floors hidden under an eight- or ten-foot layer of foodstuffs and heaps of soft, warm sacking lying about simply for the picking up. Now the tanks were empty except for the heaps of rusting, useless junk piled in the corners, and the small area in Seven where their remaining store of food was kept. With lighting restricted to three tanks, the two remaining gardens were needed for photosynthesis rather than to eke out their dwindling food supply. Then there were the light bulbs and the increasingly difficult jobs of processing drinking water and finding lubrication for the generator.

But these were all the old, accepted, everyday problems. The doctor was aware that the ship, like everyone in it, would die someday. But no sane person—and the inhabitants of *Gulf Trader* were sane, the Game saw to that —would ruin his or her whole life by worrying over the last few minutes of it. In actual fact there was nothing for any of them to complain about.

Altogether this was a happy, exciting time to be living in, and at nineteen James Eichlan Wallis felt very glad that he had been born when he had.

The target sun was so close that the small telescope in the flagship was able to resolve the tiny blurs representing its planets. But the framework of the infinitely larger and more sensitive instrument, so vast that its construction was possible only in the weightless conditions of space, was taking form between the two ships. A slightly smaller edition of the great telescope which had been set up so long ago in the doomed Unthan system to search space for a second home for their race, it would be capable, when the silvered plastic film of its reflector had been stretched into place, of resolving individual waves on the oceans of the third planet. With this bigger telescope they would obtain detailed charts of the land and sea areas, and with the aid of information sent back from the high-acceleration probes already shooting ahead of them they would choose their landing areas.

Meanwhile the position of every unit of the great fleet would have to be checked and, if necessary, corrected. The control and guidance system that would allow them to apply thrust simultaneously to each and every ship had to be tested, as did the master controls for the general warming-up prior to landing. The landing itself would be the responsibility of the original crew, but *they* would not be warmed until everything was ready for them.

The feelings of Captain Heglenni and her trainee crew towards the deep-sleeping bodies of Captain Gunt, Astrogator Gerrol, and the others were somewhat mixed. They felt a respect close to religious awe for these legendary beings who had actually lived and gone through their training on Untha itself, but there was also a feeling that came very close to being one of dislike.

Heglenni felt ashamed of this feeling. Yet, at the same time she could not help remembering that Captain Gunt had cooled himself leaving the original Deslann and Hellahar with a terrible problem to solve. When she would return the command of the flagship and the fleet to Captain Gunt, the solution to that terrible problem, she was determined, should be as complete as possible in every detail. The answer had cost so much in time and suffering and often violent death that she felt it only right that Gunt should be made to feel a little bit ashamed.

From the moment when his brain had thawed sufficiently to allow the electrochemical processes of thought to proceed normally, the newly warmed Captain Gunt had been bombarded by reports. To begin with there had been the data in the captain's log, the more detailed information relayed via Gerrol regarding Deslann's proposed solution, and the other captain's final personal message to him, and then had come the highly compressed history in the form of a report by the female Captain Heglenni, whose mere presence was proof that Deslann's solution had worked, had just reached its shattering conclusion.

There was a quality of madness about the whole situation, Gunt thought wildly: the familiar rendered frightening by a touch of the strange, the good wrecked by the bad, and joy flowing too closely to despair. The psychologists had spoken warningly about vacillation of feelings like this!

Gerrol insisted that the few errors committed on the ship had been sociological rather than technical—for the computer room around them blazed with ready signals and the navigation and course corrections of the flagship and fleet had been performed with great efficiency although the atmosphere of the room, whose water had been recycled for nearly sixteen generations, had become unpleasant to the point of nausea. The few sociological, and no doubt unavoidable, errors had begun with the catastrophic rule of Helltag the Mad and the split that left half the flagship's crew no choice but to transfer to the nearby food ship. The severity of the punishments given out to the heretics who had defied the first Deslann's edict against warming other cold-sleeping Unthans and the war between Deslann Five and Hellseggorn of the food ship, which had given the flagship a desperately needed reserve of non-sterile males, were further errors. The generations, too, of increasingly psychotic and physically malformed crew people, the sickness and suffering and often needless deaths were all a product of these errors, as was this small, lean, angry female captain.

She was waiting for him to speak.

"We have arrived safely at the target system," Gunt said stupidly. "It should be a time of great joy. Are you sure that . . . that—"

He broke off, thinking that since Heglenni had first begun her report he had been trying desperately to see some tiny resemblance to Deslann and Hellahar in this female, but in vain. If anything she reminded him of some of the early predators who had been hunted and starved out of existence when civilization had been spreading through the seas of Untha. They also had been thin, stunted, diseased, and savage.

"The telescope will fall ahead of us once thrust is applied," said Heglenni impatiently. "If you distrust my data there is still time to view the planet directly instead of studying my photographs."

"I trust your data," said Gunt dully. "The news has come as a shock to me. I was thinking aloud and perhaps hoping for a miracle."

The other captain's expression softened briefly, and for a moment Gunt thought he saw a little of Healer Hellahar's compassion and Deslann's dedication show through, then she went on, "I understand your feelings of shock and disappointment, since I share them myself, sir. The target system has been reached safely and the problem you set Captain Deslann has been solved. But the target world is inhabited more so than it was centuries ago when our original pictures were taken, when there was no evidence of widespread mechanization or road systems. It has become densely populated by an intelligent, gas-breathing form of life sufficiently advanced to cross interplanetary space. There are bases on the target planet's moon and on the dehydrated fourth planet, also strong indications of bases on the moons of the inner gas giant, planet Five. I myself can conceive of no solution to this problem nor can any of my crew, so I'm passing responsibility back to you, sir."

Neither captain spoke for a long time after that. Then slowly Captain Gunt performed the gesture of respect between equals and said formally, "I hereby relieve you of the command of this ship."

XX

The target world continued to circle her parent sun, a planet of great beauty and serenity whose peace was now actual as well as apparent. The closest and most detailed examination showed no evidence of war, the few smoke palls on the dayside being the by-product of industry while on the nightside the cities blazed only with street lights and advertising. There was still a great deal of suffering and death, but this was in distressed areas like India and China where there was, as there always had been, a shortage of food. And in a tiny bay on the southwest coast of Spain, cut off from land and sea alike by high cliffs and reefs which were thought to be impassable, in two hundred feet of water there lay a distressed area nobody knew about.

Commander James Eichlan Wallis of *Gulf Trader* (he had been elected commander as well as ship's doctor because of his seniority and a recent tendency, shared by the very first commander and all who had followed him, to worry much more than was normal about the future) was lecturing on the evils of marriage.

"There was a time in the not too distant past," he was saying in the bitter, sarcastic tones which had become second nature to him these days, "when marriage was considered a necessary evil. And a time before that, the Game tells us, when it was not considered evil at all but a necessity for a stable and happy existence. That happy state of affairs no longer obtains. Now if a man *likes* a girl, or vice versa, there is danger. For him to make love to her is nothing short of criminal insanity, the ultimate in selfishness and deliberate murder!"

"Let's change the subject, sir," said Heather May Dickson, in a voice both respectful and impatient. Her twin sister's voice was merely impatient as she said,

151

"You've told us about childbirth before, Doctor, many times—"

"And I'll tell you again!" Wallis snapped. He went on, "We lack medical facilities, food, clothing, and proper living conditions for both mother and child. The cold and damp has worsened steadily over the past few years, with the result that all of you young people have heart conditions and lung conditions which would be considered grave in a normal, well-fed, and clothed person who was not being subjected to any physical strain. You are not well fed. You are shockingly deficient in certain vitamins and your resistance to disease or infection is practically non-existent—and this is in relation to conditions within the ship only ten years ago, not the physical norm which my medical knowledge describes! Neither of you girls could survive a pregnancy, and for a baby to survive in the present living conditions would be likewise impossible. This is fact, not supposition. There are only seven of us left and we can't afford to lose anyone else—"

"If we don't marry we won't gain anyone, either," someone said *sotto voce*. It sounded like Henry Joe-Jim Dickson. The four young people laughed, but not the seniors.

The doctor said furiously, "I have in mind a modification to the Game. The idea is that instead of recalling and re-enacting scenes from Hornblower or landings on alien planets we delve into something a little closer to home: the memories of your fathers and myself, for instance, of the period immediately preceding and following your births.

"Myself, I can remember this material quite vividly," the doctor went on harshly, "even without the mental discipline of the Game. I could recall the complete medical situation as well as describe the incidental sights and, uh, sounds. Your fathers' memories will also be clear in this period, since they became widowed within a few minutes of your being born. . . ."

He had meant to shock some sense into them and the silence that followed his threat showed he might have succeeded. The other two seniors were not a problem: they were trying hard to forget the manner in which their

152

respective wives had died. On the other hand, the twin girls and the two young men, sixteen and nineteen years old, had not been there at the time so far as memory was concerned, so they *were* a problem. Warnings continually repeated tended to lose their meaning; they became, instead, tiresome rather than frightening. So the doctor was threatening in order to bring home to everyone the full, terrible meaning behind his warnings, and was using the Game to do it.

It was only a threat, of course. The thought of his ever having to put it into effect was enough to make Doctor Wallis himself start to shake.

The Game was not only sacred, it was as much a part of life in the ship as eating and breathing. During the Game life became tolerable, and even exciting and happy. It allowed them to forget the short period of nightmare each day when they walked barefoot over cold metal harsh with rust, shivering in the scraps of hair and plant fiber they called clothing.

They could forget the generator, now more a means of keeping warm than a device for supplying light, and the garden which, with insufficient light and no heat at all, barely kept itself alive. It allowed them to forget the food, still inadequate despite their having overcome their repugnance at eating the fish caught in Richard's Hole, and the damp, frigid air which tied up their muscles and joints with rheumatism and fibrositis and made their heads pound with the pain of inflamed sinuses and neuralgia and toothache. The Game allowed them to forget their shivering, wasted, and diseased bodies in the hard and sustained exercise of their minds—minds which, although they had no way of knowing it, were in many respects the keenest and most highly developed on the whole planet. That their wonderful Game should be used to remember all the things they were trying so desperately to forget was the ultimate sacrilege, an idea so perverted and horrifying that it should have been unthinkable.

But the doctor had thought of it because something drastic in the way of warnings was needed to keep the young people from mating. On the whole, life in *Gulf Trader* was bearable and providing there were no more deaths in childbirth or similar disasters, morale would remain good. They were having an unusually cold and, judging by the agitated state of the surface above them, very stormy winter. Conditions were bound to improve soon. They could hardly get any worse.

Well above the plane of the ecliptic and on the point of passing within the orbit of the system's inner gas giant, the leading elements of the Unthan fleet were decelerating and converging on the target world. Far behind them on the outermost fringe of the system, from where the sun appeared only as an unusually bright star, the main body of the fleet also decelerated and slowly converged. In the flagship most of the major decisions had already been taken, but there was discussion, argument, and recrimination regarding them.

"I agree that it is unfortunate they have attained such a high degree of civilization," Gunt was saying angrily. "If they had been backward we could simply have landed in their oceans and taken our time over making contact. With luck there might have been peaceful coexistence between us. As it is, what we are doing is bound to appear as an act of war, a large-scale invasion, and they are bound to react to it as such. Even if we had the fuel reserves to put the fleet into orbit while we tried to communicate with them, I doubt very much whether we could convince them of our peaceful intentions in the presence of such a multitude of ships!"

"It *is* their planet, sir," said Gerrol.

"We don't want all of it," one of the engineers joined in. "Just the oceans, and they don't use them for anything but floating boats on."

"This point has been raised before," Gunt resumed sharply, "by everyone including myself! The answer is ethically unsatisfactory, but it is this. If we had been the kind of race which accepted fate quietly and philosophically we would have stayed on Untha while our seas boiled away and us with them. We aren't and we didn't. This is a fight for the survival of our race, and as senior captain of the fleet my duty is clear. It is unfortunate that we are forced into fighting other intelligent beings, potentially

154

friendly beings perhaps, and that the struggle to survive in a strange environment has become a war with no foreseeable end. But we must fight and we must put every effort into fighting effectively; otherwise we might just as well have stayed at home—"

"I still think we should try to communicate, sir," another voice broke in. Inevitably it belonged to the senior communications officer, Dasdahar.

"So do I," said the captain. "But how much success have you had up to now?"

Dasdahar hesitated, then said, "These beings are gas-breathers living on the dry surface of their planet. This being so they could be expected to discover the principles of radio communication at a much earlier stage of their technological history than water-breathers like ourselves, who knew nothing about ionization layers until we were practically on the brink of space travel. The point I'm trying to make is that there are bound to be fundamental differences in approach. Add to that the fact that their aural and vocal senses are designed for use in a gaseous medium while we hear and speak through water and you will understand some of the difficulties.

"At the moment we are working on a device to convert sound waves produced in water into frequencies which should, we hope, be audible in the more tenuous gaseous medium," the officer went on. "And vice versa, of course. The tests are promising, and once we gain some idea of the frequencies used by these beings we should be able to hear them and they us. We won't be able to understand what they're *saying,* of course, but with luck maybe . . . some kind of . . . simple message . . ."

Dasdahar floundered into silence, and Gunt said, "Something more definite than an untried sound converter and a lot of wishful thinking is required if we are to change our plans, plans which have general, if reluctant, agreement. . . . And now I want to go into the landing drill in more detail. . . ."

The plan called for no change in procedure so far as the expendables were concerned. Domestic and food animals making up the vanguard would be warmed automatically just prior to arrival and released from their ships as soon as the vessels had water around them, after which they would have to fend for themselves. They would at the very least create a diversion and some might even survive. The timers throughout the fleet would be set to warm up the cold-sleeping Unthans to have the situation explained to them by Gunt and his crew on the flagship and by various sub-fleet commanders via radio on the other ships. Ideally the explanations should be given soon enough before arrival for the situation to be grasped but not so early that a general panic could develop. There were no alternatives except fight or die, and if they were going to survive as a race they would have to fight hard.

"I don't want to hear any more talk about communicating with these beings," Gunt went on harshly. "We must be realistic. They are alien people, so much so that they may have nothing in common with us. Even if we did by some chance share a common outlook or philosophy or even a dislike for something there will be no time to find out about it. To them our arrival is an act of war and in the interests of survival we must proceed as if it *is* war!

"The landing areas have been chosen with concealment and survival in mind," the captain went on, "such as near outcroppings of rock which penetrate the surface and similar obstacles to sea-surface navigation, underwater caves and geological features where we can establish concealed bases. The data from the probes and the telescopic observations will enable the fleet to land in optimum surroundings. The water is breathable so that no cumbersome protective suits will be needed. . . ."

Immediately as a ship landed, its newly warmed cargo would scatter, carrying as much portable equipment as possible. Later, if the ship were not destroyed in some fashion by the enemy, they might risk returning for heavier and more complex equipment, but only if it were safe to do so. The main idea was to hide and survive until their strange new world no longer seemed so strange. Very likely a great number of them would be hunted down and killed, but not everyone. Some of them would survive and go on the offensive. In time there might even be peace.

Nevertheless, at the present time the most important point to remember was that the new world was almost as strange to the enemy as it was to themselves. The planet belonged to these gas-breathers and they floated thousands of surface vessels on its oceans, and there were many indications that they were not afraid of water, but as a race they did not live and breathe in water, they did not have the instincts or the evolutionary background of the Unthans. It was the captain's belief that many more of his people would survive than would be killed.

Which brought him to the subject of weapons.

" . . . The weapon most likely to be used against us," Gunt continued, "will be a limited mass-destruction affair using a chemical charge exploded at depth and relying on compression effects to produce casualties. We may expect a great many of these bombs to reach us, singly and in patterns calculated to inflict maximum damage. Our defense against this weapon will be our high degree of mobility, early decentralization, and small personnel domes anchored to the sea bed using layers of plastic, gas, and gas-filled sponge to absorb the shock waves. At the present time I do not see them exploding nuclear weapons in the sea, as our observations regarding their population and the numbers of small surface vessels indicate that the sea might be a small but important part of their food supply. They will not want to risk poisoning it until their position appears desperate.

"Our own weapons will be crude and ineffectual to begin with," the captain went on. "Spring-loaded harpoons, a few adhesive mines, and so on. If the gas-breathers underestimate us, so much the better. Eventually some of us will establish ourselves, reclaim heavy equipment from our abandoned ships, begin mining the sea bed. Quietly we will develop more sophisticated weapons, process radioactives, perfect our technology. We will stockpile dirigible torpedoes carrying nuclear warheads capable of traversing the gas envelope and striking any point on the planetary surface.

"The pollution of the planet's gas envelope and the death of surface food supplies will have very little effect on sea dwellers," Gunt went on grimly, "and provided we retain the initiative, retaliation from the gas-breathers should be minimal."

There was a strange lack of motion in the bodies around him, and he was aware that the silence was not simply due to attention for a superior officer. Astrogator Gerrol, the engineers, and the rest of his contemporary crew members were floating still and silent like so many cooled food animals, all staring at him with exactly the same expression. Even the female Heglenni, who, because of her lack of sensitivity and background, might have been expected to support him, wore the same expression.

Gunt did not try to meet their eyes. Angrily, he said, "It's them, or us. I'm sorry, it is a question of survival!"

XXI

Conditions, Doctor Wallis had been fond of telling his people, could not possibly get worse. . . .

They were awakened one night in late winter, that is, those who were lucky enough to be asleep, by a high-pitched creaking noise and the sound of running water. There had never been sounds like this in living memory or in the Game-recalled history of the ship, so they struggled out of their sleeping hair and ran for'ard, following the direction of the noises. They ran fast and sure-footed despite the darkness, because they knew every inch of the way, the height and placing of every watertight door, and the exact position of the contents of each and every tank. It was a matter of memory plus the fact that there had been no changes in the ship for a very long time. Now, however, there was change.

In Number Four they ran into water, a slow, icy trickle moving aft along the deck and collecting, because of the stern-downward attitude of the ship, at the watertight door between Four and Five. At the entrance to Three the water was dammed up level with the coaming and they splashed through it knee-deep. It was the same beyond the entrance to One, except that here the water poured over the edge of the coaming in a steady flood, and from the forward wall of the tank there came sounds as of a gentle waterfall overlaid by the erratic creaking and groaning of metal under strain. The deck beneath their feet seemed to twitch and shiver.

"Everybody out!" shouted the doctor. "There's nothing here worth salvaging. *Out!*"

Wallis stationed himself at the watertight door, counting the bodies as they went past him. He had no idea who they were exactly since they were merely centers of heavy breathing and splashing in the darkness, but five of them went through before the forward wall gave. There was a sharp, metallic screech, a gargantuan bubbling and then by a sudden rush of water he was swept through the door gasping and trying not to cry out with the pain of what the rusty edge of the door had done to the skin of his hip and leg. Then, abruptly, the flood was gone as suddenly as it had come. Wallis picked himself up and moved to examine the door.

Despite the stiff, rust-clogged hinges the weight of water pouring into Number One had slammed the door shut. But the door, again because of rust, was no longer completely watertight. The doctor's exploring fingers detected a thin, high-pressure jet of water coming from the edge of the door all the way round. The plating between the flooded One and Two was beginning to creak alarmingly under the mounting pressure of water, and above them the escaping air thumped and gurgled thunderously towards the weather deck and the surface. Everywhere there was the pattering and splashing of water.

"Back to Four!" called the doctor. "Forget about Two and Three. But make sure the door is tight. Scrape off the rust, hammer it loose, do what you can. And *hurry*!"

Two and Three were saddle tanks and if one should remain airtight while the other did not, there would be a strain set up in the badly weakened fabric of the ship, a strain which might very well crack open the entire system of tanks. Allowing both tanks to flood would equalize the strain on the forward wall of Four. It would also, Wallis reminded himself, double it!

Like the other watertight doors between the tanks, this one had been dogged open to facilitate the free circulation of air, and like the others it was practically rusted solid in that position. They had to hammer at the door and its surrounding with scrap metal in an effort to dislodge the gritty incrustation that could be felt (but could not be seen) covering everything, then to scrape frantically with bits of metal and wood and even their fingers to free hinges and coaming of the clogging rust. They used files that were themselves little more than bars of rust and the damage they inflicted on each other amid the darkness and confusion was severe although not, it

160

seemed, immediately disabling. Yet, all the time the water rose steadily, spraying into Four through the supposedly watertight door from Two. When they closed the door they were working on to check the fit, water built up so quickly behind it that the efforts of all of them were needed to push it open again. Then came the time when they could not force it open. Water streamed from its edges in a steadily increasing volume and ran aft along the deck. They were forced to retreat again.

The door into Seven was in better condition, since it was closed frequently to contain the heat generated by the lighting in the garden there. Number Seven held, even though it was not perfectly tight either. Nevertheless, it allowed them time to stop and think. It gave them a chance to take stock, to realize how much was lost to them, and to adjust to their new, harsher and, it was plainly obvious, all too impermanent world.

The other two seniors were dead. The elder Dickson had been trapped in Number One and Wallis's brother had died during the confusion in Four. It was difficult to say what exactly had happened by touch alone, but it seemed that his brother had tripped in the darkness—a lot of gear had changed its position, moved both by the water and by the people working on the doors—and hit his head with sufficient force for him to lose consciousness, and he had drowned quietly in a few inches of water. They could have moved the body aft, but the doctor had asked that it be left where it was. The entrance to Richard's Hole was under water, as was the generator, the garden, and most of the bedding. All the tanks forward of Seven were flooded or inaccessible. Within the space of a few hours their world had shrunk by half.

Whereas before there had been miserable cold and dampness, there was now the added misery of flooding. The water was more than a foot deep around the connecting doors and, because of the attitude of the ship, it was almost waist-deep in the sternmost tank, Number Twelve. With the generator gone and the garden destroyed by sea water there was no possibility of producing light or heat, or of recycling air or distilling drinking water. With half their world had gone half their air supply. There were odd scraps of wood and metal, even a few electric light bulbs, and enough food. They would not starve. The food supply, while meager, would far outlast the water and air.

Full circle, thought Wallis.

Five survivors in a sunken ship, Wallis thought sadly. Two young couples and an aging, bad-tempered doctor facing death because there wasn't enough air or drinking water. But this time there was no possibility of continued survival, for their resources were gone and there was no scope in which to exercise their ingenuity, nothing with which they could build a world for themselves, and no means of extending their lives by more than a few weeks. This was, finally, the end of the world. They should all try to accept that fact, stop struggling, and try to adopt a more philosophical attitude to their approaching end.

"Is anyone badly hurt?" Wallis asked gently.

There were numerous cuts and bruises, but nothing serious. He advised them to bathe the wounds in a saline solution—there was plenty of it about—to remove dirt or rust, and warned them not to cover the areas until a scab had formed because of the danger of septicemia from the hair coverings. He also suggested that they move to Richard's Rooms with as much bedding as could be salvaged, that being the only relatively dry spot in the ship. They could wave the damp bedding around their heads to dry it off, and the exercise would help keep them warm. . . .

That night they did not play the Game. Instead they huddled together for warmth, wriggling to get closer together and farther away from the cold, damp bedding and even colder deck, which sucked the heat remorselessly from them, and cursed because they could do neither. It was the first time the Game had not been played, the first night that their phenomenal minds and tremendous memories had not been able to lift them out of the discomfort of the here-and-now and into the bright, happy worlds of music and fiction and history, even of ship history. It was the first time that the memories of recent events had raised such a terrible barrier, a barrier cutting off all retreat into the past, the future, or even the might-have-been.

It was perhaps the first time that they all realized that there was no hope, that there never had been any hope.

The commander lay shivering and cursing and listening to the sounds of dripping water and the creaking of their rusty, disintegrating world for a very long time; then he said, "You know, with five of us occupying this small cabin there is bound to be a lot of breath condensation. We can collect it and eke out the drinking water. It might even be possible to salvage enough for a small generator—a hand model, of course, because of the small space available, and, if nothing else, building it will occupy our minds. We'll have to make a determined effort to attract attention again, by banging on the hull in relays. This will help warm us up as well as . . . as . . ."

He trailed off into silence and the silence remained unbroken.

You stupid, cowardly fool! he raged silently at himself. *Don't you know when to give up!*

On the surface, in the War Room of a building many times older than the sunken tanker, other men were discussing the question of survival.

"Is it agreed that we use anti-missiles, proximity-fused, with chemical warheads?" said the officer at one side of the table. "Our anti-missiles were intended for use against ground-launched ICBMs, and will therefore not be effective until the enemy has penetrated to within one hundred miles of the surface. Do we also agree that to use nuclear warheads in these circumstances would hurt us more than the enemy, assuming that the enemy ships are in fact susceptible to damage and are not equipped with, uh, super weapons of offense or defense?"

There was no head to the table. The officers seated around it were the top military men of their respective governments and bore equal rank despite the fact that some of their uniforms were heavy with ribbons and gold braid while others were almost ostentatiously simple and unadorned. It was one of the latter who spoke next, using his interpreter.

"I do not understand their strategy," he said. "To send in a small advance force to test our defenses is good.

163

To wait nearly a year, which is the time our observatories tell us will be required for the remainder of their fleet to reach earth, before committing the main force is bad tactics. It gives us too much time to prepare."

"Not enough time, by far," said another. "With luck we will be able to deal with the first wave using all of our present stock of anti-missiles, but a year is not enough to prepare for the main invasion!"

"The whole idea of an invasion from space is tactically unsound," a quieter voice broke in. "Perhaps this is an assumption we were too quick to make. The aliens have begun to send what appear to be signals, a continuous audio-frequency note, containing patterned interruptions, like Morse in reverse. If we assume instead that . . ."

His voice was drowned suddenly in a flood of objections, which condensed after a few minutes into the quiet, sardonic voice and objections of one man.

"There is no peaceful solution to this problem, General," he said. "At their present rate of deceleration the vanguard of the enemy fleet is just fifty-six hours away. If they were broadcasting messages of peace and good will in perfect English with an accent of one of your better public schools, we could act no differently: it would be the same as saying that Overlord had been mounted so that the men could picnic on the Normandy beaches. Their presence and behavior here is plainly, unmistakably hostile."

"Our launching sites aren't positioned for an attack from space," said another voice worriedly. "But it would be good tactics for them to orbit a few times to get a closer look at their objectives, and perhaps do a little softening-up, in which case all our sites would get a crack at them as they went over. The thing bothering me is if they try to soften us up with H-bombs—"

"Not likely, I would say," another voice broke in. "The size of the fleet alone would make it seem certain that they intend landing and that they should not want to dirty up their bridgehead with fallout. Of course, we may have been under surveillance without knowing it for a long time. They might know enough about our physical make-up to use nerve gases or bacteria—"

164

"No matter what they send we'll have to soak it up," the first officer broke in. "If they come straight in so that the majority of our launchers cannot be brought to bear, we'll have to hit them with jets and ground artillery. If they become established we may be forced to use nuclear weapons, which would be very bad if the area were densely populated. But if they make the mistake of going into orbit, especially if it is a low, bombing orbit—"

" . . . We'll clobber them," someone finished for him.

The vanguard of the Unthan fleet did not go into orbit. It did not have the fuel reserves to do so. In the flagship's forward screens the surface features of the target world—layers of water vapor hanging in the gas envelope, details of the drab, useless land masses and the tremendous blue oceans—grew steadily larger and crawled over the edges of the picture. The casualties they suffered were reflected in the computer room, where lights went out quietly and guidance systems died at the other end and from where it was difficult to realize the true extent of the devastation and death taking place all around them. Looking out of the direct vision panels it was hard for Gunt to realize that anything at all was happening or that there were beings down there doing their best to kill him . . . until the detectors showed a missile climbing towards them, closing fast.

It was over so quickly that by the time his lagging brain realized that he was about to die they had been reprieved and he was free to work out what had actually happened.

Obviously the missile's target-seeker had equated size with importance and turned it at the penultimate instant onto the larger food ship, which had been keeping close station on them for so many generations. The missile must have penetrated the hull before exploding, because the ship seemed to jerk apart silently as the force of the explosion was transmitted through the water to every single corner of its structure. It opened out slowly, hurling great masses of metal, gobbets of coldly steaming water, and the twitching bodies of the food animals in all directions. Gunt cringed as several times debris narrowly

165

missed the flagship, but unknown to him, the expanding sphere of wreckage was confusing the ground radar, making it impossible to detect a whole ship among the falling pieces, so it saved his ship.

The flagship dived through the cloud layer into heavy precipitation and strong winds and near darkness, to hang poised for an instant above the storm-tossed sea before sliding quietly below the surface.

Now they would have to spend precious time hunting for shelter and hope that their movements and eventual hiding place did not register on the detecting instruments of the enemy. Gunt intended to camouflage the ship, if he had time, and arrange a system of communications, but before that happened his colonists would form into their preselected survival groups and scatter themselves up and down this rocky, beautiful subcoastline. They would not scatter too far because the captain wanted to know what to expect in the way of weapons and general nastiness from the enemy so that he, or the person who survived him, could tell the later arrivals what to expect. They were little more than experimental animals, Gunt thought sickly, being tested to destruction.

Captain Heglenni and her females had been given a much more positive assignment, that of obtaining specimens of the enemy life-form together with whatever artifacts and mechanisms became available for study. It was accepted that Heglenni would have to kill the specimens and take the mechanisms by force and that the war was only just beginning, but Captain Gunt did not allow himself to think about that too much. The future was too horrible for any sane person to dwell in it mentally for any longer than was necessary.

His ship was down, safely.

XXII

More than eighty per cent of the Unthan vanguard escaped the anti-missiles and reached the ocean safely. The earth defenses, with no previous experience of invasion from space, had deployed as best they could against expected landings in force in desert or thinly populated areas. They were thrown badly off balance by the fact that the enemy did not make a single preliminary orbit, that instead of a concentration of force they came down in single units scattered all over the surface of the globe, and that the landings did not take place on land but in the sea around the world's coastlines. Except for one ship, that was.

This one had escaped the anti-missiles to land, owing to a fault in its guidance system, in a large park in one of the larger coastal cities. It thundered down to a perfect landing less than a quarter of a mile from the water's edge, to stand like some tremendous metal lighthouse among the smoldering trees and bushes. When the echoes of its touchdown had died away and before the city could recover from its shocked silence there could be heard a muffled, erratic pounding coming from the interior of the great ship. The beings packing the refrigerated holds of the ship, warmed automatically to full consciousness on the way down, had begun to panic. Quarters which had been barely large enough to hold their frozen, unconscious bodies were now jammed solid with the normally placid food animals biting and tearing at themselves and each other in their efforts to escape.

But the mechanism that should have caused large sections of the hull to fall open and allow the beings inside the freedom of the sea refused to operate because of certain built-in safety devices. While the ship was surrounded, not by water but by a completely unbreathable gas, the opening mechanism refused to operate and the ship's hull remained tightly and stubbornly closed.

For all of six minutes . . .

That was how long it took for the jets to arrive, screaming in from tree-top height and hurling against the towering alien hull a veritable rain of armor-piercing missiles, small HE bombs, and napalm. There were certain tactical atomic weapons which could have been brought to bear, but out of consideration for the city's inhabitants lesser forms of frightfulness were being tried first. The ship stood against the onslaught for less than a minute before it burst open, toppled heavily, and began to disintegrate. The napalm fires hissed furiously and died in the torrents of water pouring from the stricken ship; and from the subsiding masses of metal, great slick-bodied alien shapes fell heaving and rolling and flapping into the steaming mud. And still the jets maintained their attack, saturating the tiny landing area with a rain of HE, tearing the ship and its contents into smaller and smaller pieces. When they finally pulled out, remade their formations, and began to circle warily, the section of the park where the enemy ship had landed had been converted into a ghastly, steaming stew of mud, riven metal, and shapeless pieces of raw meat.

It was a shock, somehow, to find that the blood of the enemy was red.

"Until the present moment," said the officer whose uniform showed dark blue between the heavy incrustations of gold, "I had thought that this was to be a space battle, with no place at all in it for the Navy. It seems I was wrong."

"As soon as they saw the ship was filled with water they should have stopped the attack!" said the gray-haired civilian who had just finished making his report. Angrily, he went on, "The beings would have died anyway, suffocated like landed fish. Now, as things are, you haven't left us with a single whole specimen. We have only the vaguest idea of their size or mass or limb arrangement, and the destruction of their ship was so thorough that its power plant was wrecked along with everything else, and now the level of radiation from the wreckage is so high that we can't get near it! Potentially the greatest scientific find in all history and we can't even—"

"The implications of a water-dwelling species who have crossed interstellar space are not lost on us, Doctor," a bespectacled officer broke in smoothly. "In their culture the attainment of space travel would represent a much greater technical achievement and would come at a much later stage of civilization—always assuming they are civilized—and would represent a double barrier to be surmounted, from sea to air or land surface, then from land or sea surface to space. Moreover, their invasion fleet would require a high degree of technical cooperation in the building, and cooperation implies civilization, although its presence here is not a civilized act—at least, not according to our ideas of civilized behavior—"

"Well now," said the civilian expert, "we've done some odd things in the name of civilization—"

"This is no time for philosophy!" another officer broke in. "These people live in the sea and they will fight in the sea. Their weapons are designed for that medium, which is probably why they took no offensive or defensive action on the way in. Our problem is that we cannot possibly interdict every square mile of ocean surface. We were lucky this time to inflict twenty per cent casualties. If we can't stop their landing, then this will be predominantly a naval war. I agree with the admiral."

"We have a little experience with the noises produced by dolphins," the bespectacled officer resumed, "which is a form of language. Also, even if we could surmount the second double barrier of air-water communications, there must be basic differences in psychology. We may have nothing in common with them at all."

"Except possibly the instinct for survival," the civilian expert put in.

"But it could be argued, Doctor, that survival in its fullest sense requires cooperation rather than conflict. If we could communicate . . ."

"You are philosophizing again," said the admiral drily, "and at present we should be dealing with the more practical aspects of this problem. We can philosophize

169

later, after we have drawn up some sort of plan to deal with this invasion. Inasmuch as only few if any of you can think in terms of naval strategy, I propose to outline the problem from my own point of view."

He glanced quickly around the table, received nods, grunts of assent, and stony silences, and then went on, "To begin with, we must assume that their main force will reach our oceans with only minor losses. They will then establish undersea bases and observation posts, and the opening stages of the war will involve action between our surface craft and submarines and the vessels and weapons of the enemy. Even though we will be fighting in our own oceans, I'm afraid the enemy will be more at home in them than we are, so to begin with our casualties will be heavy and the enemy will seem to have things all his own way. This situation will change, however, as we gain experience of their weapons, tactics, physical and mental capabilities.

"Acquiring dead specimens and live prisoners is of immediate importance," he continued, looking steadily at the bespectacled officer. "If at all possible we must communicate with them. We must know the enemy.

"With this knowledge," he resumed to the table in general, "we will be in a position to hunt down the enemy and try to exterminate him completely. I say 'try to' deliberately because I don't think it possible to kill each and every one of them. But we must aim to keep them from becoming established to the point where they can take the offensive against us by launching missiles from the sea bed, and so on. Also, from the admittedly cursory examination of enemy remains made by the doctor here I think it safe to assume that these beings are not capable of surviving at great depths, which means that they will tend to congregate near coastlines and in other fairly shallow areas. This simplifies the job of detecting and destroying their installations, but it will in no sense make the job easy. This is going to be a long, hard, and undecisive war.

"Even with perfect communication between both sides," he went on grimly, "I see no way of stopping it. The situation has deteriorated beyond the possibility of peaceful settlement since their leading contingent has already been attacked and suffered heavy casualties. What I propose is the mounting of a maximum effort operation against this relatively weak force of the enemy before the main force of the enemy arrives, in an attempt to devise and perfect tactics suited to a form of warfare which will be utterly strange to us."

He paused briefly for comment, then went on, "If we assume this initial landing to have been a test of our defenses and an attempt to gather on-the-spot intelligence regarding us, we are going to encounter the enemy close inshore—at least, to begin with. It should be no problem to detect a large mass of metal the size and shape of the enemy ships with the detection gear already available to us; however, the Western Approaches, the Med, and large areas of the Pacific are practically carpeted with masses of metal the shape and size of the enemy ships—the naval and merchant-shipping losses of World War Two. In a very short time we can expect the enemy to put these relics to good use, as forward observation posts in the shallows and for purposes of camouflage at greater depths—two masses of metal lying close together on the sea bed being difficult to distinguish from one. Even the metal of a small sunken vessel would serve to screen the weapons and smaller transport vehicles of an enemy patrol, so our first step must be to depth-bomb each and every sunken hulk around our coastlines, and to do so repeatedly at the shortest possible intervals.

"The compression effects of a large explosion would undoubtedly kill anyone sheltering in or near a wreck," he went on quickly, answering the questions which several of them were about to ask, "but two weeks later, or even hours later, it would still be there and available for use as a shelter or screen for enemy metal. So every wreck or suspicious mass of metal that it is possible to detect will be hit repeatedly with depth bombs—chemical explosives, of course, unless we suspect a concentration of enemy in the area—"

"Just a minute, sir," said the officer with the glasses, whose specialty was communications. "The population is such that we depend on offshore fishing to a large extent for food. If we contaminate the sea with radioactives . . .

171

As well as killing the fish there is the problem of evapo-
ration and later precipitation over land. You're going to
make this a very dirty war, sir."

"Yes," said the admiral, "a long, dirty war."

The fighter bomber hugged the tops of the waves all
the way to the target area, then climbed slightly, pivoted
its jets, and slid to a stop two hundred feet above a marker
placed there by a fast detector boat. The boat had
dropped a magnet to which was attached a line and a
quantity of marker dye, and had then left in a hurry.
It was said now that the Navy expected torpedoes to
come straight up at them, so their lookouts used glass-
bottomed buckets instead of binoculars. A heavy depth
charge splashed into the sea where it was stained yellow by
the marker. A few minutes later the surface turned white,
bulged upward, and slowly subsided to leave a great,
pale, circular stain where once there had been a tiny
yellow one.

"That's the second time this month we've hit that thing,
whatever it is," said the navigator-bombardier. "It's
not very exciting or dramatic, is it? I keep expecting to
see wreckage or bodies floating up."

"After 150 years," said the pilot, "any loose wood or
bedding would be too waterlogged to rise. The only bodies
you could expect to see would be concussed fish or
aliens."

"But for argument's sake suppose we saw *human* bodies
floating up. . . ."

"Don't be ridiculous! Much more of these morbid
imaginings and I'll sic the station psychologist onto you.
Now, the next wreck on the list is that tanker off Ber-
trand's Head. Give me a course, please."

The inhabited world of *Gulf Trader* had shrunk to
the two cabins comprising Richard's Rooms and the upper
half of Number Twelve tank. It was a cold, dank, dying
world, shivering and starving and strangling in its own
waste products. The air was fresher near the roof of
Number Ten, but nobody wanted to take the risk of diving into the inky water of Twelve, groping their way

through the submerged door, and swimming up to the surface in Ten just for the sake of breathing air which did not
stink.

Instead they huddled together in their pile of damp and
filthy hair, trying to talk themselves into starting a Game
but more often keeping silent except for the chattering of
their teeth. During daylight they watched the scummed-
over porthole waiting for something, anything, to happen.
Then one day, incredibly, it did.

"A sh-shadow!" chattered one of the girls. "It was
moving slowly, up there! Didn't you s-see it?"

"I saw something," said Wallis. "It might be a big fish.
Or-r a boat on the surface. . . ."

There was a sudden, muted clang and a scraping sound,
subtly different from all the other metallic creakings and
strainings which haunted the ship.

"A boat on the surface," said Wallis, in a voice which
began as a whisper and ended as a shout, "has dropped
its anchor on us!"

Within seconds they were all banging furiously on the
cabin deck and walls, in unison, with the first piece of
metal or wood that came to hand. *Bang-bang-bang,* they
signaled hysterically, *bang, bang, bang, bang-bang-bang.*
They did not speak at all among themselves, because it
was ridiculous to expect rescue after all this time and
talking about the possibility would have made them realize
just *how* ridiculous it was. Instead they banged away while
the minutes grew into hours and they grew warmer than
they could ever remember being from their exertions, then
cold again as they weakened. During the lengthening
pauses for breath they stared through the green scum on
the other side of the porthole and imagined moving shadows, or listened to the odd creakings and scrapings and
gurgling sounds coming from different parts of the ship,
and tried to convince themselves that they were not the
same noises they always heard.

"It might have been part of the mast breaking away,"
said Wallis, during one of the longer silences. "A piece
of rusty metal falling onto the deck . . ."

They ignored him. Weakly, despairingly, they resumed

hammering on the deck. Then suddenly they stopped. Light was seeping into the cabin from the tank below.

Wallis and one of the girls were first to the hatch and gained a place on the ladder while the others knelt in the cabin above, staring down, punching each other and laughing. Below him the water was lit by a lamp of some kind which was being pushed through the submerged entrance. A shape in some kind of diving suit was following it, and obviously having difficulty squeezing through. It was impossible to see details because the water was like so much cold, thick, stinking soup with the wastes that had collected in it over the past few weeks. Wallis felt suddenly anxious about their rescuer's feelings over this, and about his people's appearance and what he should say. "Hello" or "Thank God" or "You certainly took your time getting here, friend. . . ."

The figure broke the surface and Wallis saw that the helmet was designed to keep water in and air out, and that the . . . head . . . inside it was not human.

XXIII

The first tape from the former Captain Heglenni said, "It is one of their larger vessels sunk, judging by the advanced state of corrosion, more than one hundred of this planet's years ago. While investigating we were startled to hear noises emanating from it in a patterned sequence suggesting intelligence, and later discovered living gas-breathers in one of the gas pockets inside the vessel. I will repeat, there were five living gas-breathers inside the ship. After seeing me, there was a surprisingly short period of adjustment on their part, after which one of them drew signs on the powdered corrosion covering a wall. One appeared to be a geometrical design illustrating Trennochalin's theorem regarding the area of squares on a right-angled triangle and the other was a nonscale diagram of this solar system. It seems to me that contact is possible with these gas-breathers and, if so, much useful information both physical and psychological could be gained regarding them, especially since they must be totally unaware of the situation between our race and theirs. I hereby request that a communications officer be assigned to me, preferably the one who was trying to develop the sound conversion device.

"With this report I am returning a dead gas-breather. This specimen appears to have died from water strangulation rather than from disease or injury. It was in a water-filled compartment of the ship and seems to have died recently. Small native predators have been at work on the specimen, but the bone structure and major organs appear to be intact. . . ."

Captain Gunt allowed the tape to run to its conclusion before turning to the communications officer, who hung like an iridescent shadow in the darkened control room. Because of the risk of detection there was no power source operating within the ship, no lighting and no water-circulating machinery. The water they breathed was that of the sea outside, gloriously cool, at a comfortable pressure and so free of salts, unlike the water of Untha, that its effects came close to that of euphoria. This was how Untha must have been before their sun began to boil off and thicken their water. This fresh, cold, tremendous ocean came close to being the Unthan conception of Heaven. It was an effort, sometimes, to realize that this perfect place had to be fought for and that the fight would be long and hard. That when they won, if they won, this gloriously clean sea might very well be left poisoned with radiation and dirtier even than the steaming seas of Untha.

Angrily, Gunt said, "I won't order you to this duty, and it's quite obvious that you would probably desert if I tried to stop your going. Just please remember that you are not going merely to satisfy your curiosity regarding a nonhuman intelligent life-form. Your only purpose is to gain information about the enemy that will aid our survival and hasten their demise. A great many of our people are going to die shortly and the quantity and accuracy of this information will be in inverse proportion to the casualties. My original plan was to disperse the colonists as soon and as far as possible. Tell Heglenni that I now intend holding them close to the ship until the last possible moment so that they can scatter into their survival cells with all the available data on the enemy.

"Tell her that her background will fit her for this duty," Gunt went on awkwardly. "It will make her less squeamish regarding the methods of getting this vital information. Tell her also that we are very pleased with her, and that I consider this matter of such importance that I will have a line laid connecting the flagship with the wreck of the enemy. It will be a sound line, since vision would be superfluous and radio would be open to detection from above. . . ."

The second report was more in the nature of a discussion, since Gunt was in a position to comment on the data as they arrived. It seemed that the five gas-breathers were close to death from starvation, suffocation, and something else which apparently had to do with breathing, or

176

perhaps swallowing, small quantities of water through their oral openings. Heglenni had dealt with the first problem by trapping for them a selection of small fish and crustaceans and with the second by floating pipes to the surface, during darkness so as to conceal the operation as much as possible, and replacing the foul gas inside the wreck. The third problem was more difficult since the gas-breathers refused to breathe or eat clean water brought to them from the sea outside their ship and refused it with the same degree of firmness as they had the water contaminated with their wastes. Since they had been able to survive for so long in these conditions, Heglenni was concerned and puzzled over what it was that they lacked. She intended carrying out a thorough search of the recently flooded compartments of the wreck in the hope of finding food supplies or mechanisms which might give a clue to what was missing.

The report which followed a few days later was more emotional than was called for, Gunt thought. She told him that the gas-breathers were in a severely weakened state and were scarcely able to communicate, even among themselves. The old male gas-breather—there were three males and two females—was in a pitiable condition. Had the captain any suggestions?

"I have, as a matter of fact," Gunt replied after some hesitation. "From observations on the way in, together with a study of the artifacts you sent us, particularly a small, electrically heated container used for warming water—a container much too small for cooking purposes and wired in such a way that the contents would tend to become vaporized rather than simply warmed—we have evolved a rather, uh, wild theory to the effect that the water used by the gas-breathers is exclusively the result of precipitation from water vapor in the planetary gas envelope. Water thus produced would be much freer from impurities like dissolved minerals and salts; so sea water might be toxic to them. This is, uh, my theory and as I've already said, it has a low order of probability."

"It certainly has!" Heglenni burst in. "But we'll try it. We'll try *anything!*"

Gunt held onto his temper with an effort, thinking unkind things about overemotional females. He said, "Meanwhile, if one or more of the specimens die you will transfer the bodies to the flagship without delay—"

"That may be difficult, sir," Dasdahar, the communications officer, broke in. "Our present contact with them is in a delicate state. We are gaining their trust, and withdrawing one of their dead could very well spoil everything."

"You surprise me," said Gunt. "I assumed that you knew only a few words of each other's language and that the rest of your knowledge regarding them was based on observation and intuition, the latter being supplied by Heglenni, whose dormant maternal instincts have been aroused by feelings of pity for her pets! Can you actually make yourselves understood in their language?"

"No, yes, sir," said Dasdahar. "What I mean, sir, is that we can make ourselves understood in *our* language. You see, the vocal apparatus of the gas-breathers is much more flexible than our own plus the fact that their memory is unusually retentive. They never forget anything that is told to them, even if it is only once. Quite complicated concepts were being exchanged in Unthan before they became too weakened to talk to us."

"But now we are going to revive them with distilled water!" Heglenni's voice added scornfully, "We respectfully end message, sir."

Using one of the cutting torches and an uninhabited gas pocket in the forward part of the wreck, Heglenni produced a fair quantity of distilled water and introduced it via a screw-topped container to the quarters of the gas-breathers. The effects were almost immediate and quite dramatic. But Heglenni observed the gas-breathers, and Dasdahar and she talked to them for a full day before contacting Captain Gunt again.

"Distilled water was the answer, sir," she said. "And for my disrespectful remarks and behavior yesterday I am truly sorry."

"Contact is widening, sir," said Dasdahar. "I have additional data for you. . . ."

And day after day the information continued to flow

into the flagship at a steadily accelerating rate. The reason for the specimens' unusually retentive memories became plain: for more than one hundred of the planet's years the dwellers in the wreck had had nothing to do *but* exercise their memories! Most of the data had to do with life in the wreck, but there was an enormous amount of information regarding the world as it had been before their ship had been rendered nonbuoyant—data on the arts as well as technology, data which gave depth and perspective to the gas-breather's culture. And through it all there was emerging the personality of Wah-Lass, the oldest specimen, who was the gas-breathing equivalent of a healer.

All the material was interesting and a fair proportion of it was useful. With the remainder of the Unthan fleet crossing the orbit of the fourth planet and with his final instructions to those ships still to go out, Captain Gunt was interested only in what was useful.

Two of the invading life-forms were captured, intact if not alive. One had been harpooned and the other machine-gunned and both were nearly torn to pieces by a ravening horde of the world's most eminent biologists eager for the chance of seeing what made the extraterrestrials tick. But when the investigation was finally carried out they were left feeling more puzzled than ever, because it appeared that the two specimens belonged to different subspecies, that the tentacles which ringed their head sections were not capable of fine manipulation and that their cranial capacity was rather small in proportion to their size, roughly that of a small whale. They would have liked to have issued a statement to the effect that the specimens in question did not have the brainpower to develop tools or the dexterity to use them, but they had to be cautious because the specimens were, after all, alien.

Meanwhile the armed forces of the world, unable to check the coming invasion, welded themselves more and more closely together and tried to perfect tactics designed to exterminate the enemy when he was down. One of them, the rapid detection and depth-bombing of sunken ships, was well-nigh perfect.

179

There was fresh food every day in the shape of fish and lobsters, and fresh air was piped directly from the surface every night. Their living quarters had been extended, they had a much better view, and there was even heat of a kind. The heat came from the Unthan equivalent of an acetylene burner, a gadget so powerful that it had to be directed downward into the water in Number Twelve to keep it from burning a hole through the plating. The result was a hot fog when it was working and a cold, clammy dampness when it was not.

Wallis had begun to cough a lot recently. He had other chest symptoms and sometimes a temperature which made him feel quite delirious.

It was time that he asked Heglenni, or the other one, who worked the sound-converter gadget, to put them ashore again. The first time he had asked, Heglenni had avoided the question by pretending not to understand and the doctor had not pushed it. The e-ts had saved their lives, after all, and Heglenni had wanted to learn more about the humans and she could not do this if her pet gas-breather, as she called him, was somewhere on land. She insisted that the humans and she had a great deal in common, and so had the male Unthan who was a communications officer on their ship. There was also the fact that up to now Wallis had been scared stiff of being brought to the surface. His world had been *Gulf Trader* and the surface was suddenly, now that it was within reach, as strange and frightening as the world of the afterlife. The others felt much the same way, so nobody had pushed the matter. Now, however, Wallis knew he would not live much longer if he stayed here.

Maybe it was due partly to his delirium and partly to his nasty, suspicious mind, but he found himself wondering about the motives of his rescuers, if rescuers they were going to be. The language wasn't much of a problem these days, although some of the growly words still made him cough, so he was pretty sure that he did not mistake the things being said to him. Ambiguity was one thing and a downright inconsistency was another. While it was understandable that the Unthans switched out their lights at night and piped in fresh air during darkness (Wallis had received, or been given, the impression that Heglenni's ship had carried refugees fleeing from some catastrophe on the home world and they were being cautious about revealing themselves until they knew more about the place), there was still something odd about the way they refused to go into details regarding themselves.

The Game had dealt with many variations on this particular theme: good aliens, bad aliens, bad aliens pretending to be good, and so on. Wallis felt very much ashamed of himself, because he would have been dead several months ago if it hadn't been for Heglenni, but he thought that the time had come to set a few verbal traps.

He knew enough of the language, and provided he didn't cough too much when he was growling out the words and could keep his mind clear when his temperature was going into a peak, he should be able to find out what he wanted to know.

But what *did* he want to know?

It was at times like this, when he looked through a fog of delirium at the rusty bulkheads and the weird orange light-rod and the nightmare features of Heglenni as she hovered outside the extension to Richard's Rooms, that he wondered seriously whether or not this was *all* delirium and his pneumonia was farther advanced than he realized.

" . . . You stupid, irresponsible fools!" Gunt's voice raged at them over the line. "How could you be so . . . so . . . What have *you* to say about this?"

Dasdahar looked helplessly at Heglenni and prepared to give the softest answer possible.

"We don't know why the gas-breathers became suspicious of us, sir," he said quickly, "but they did, and quite suddenly became uncooperative. We were in the process of obtaining some very useful information and we took the decision to tell them—"

"I took the decision," said Heglenni sharply. "The fault is entirely mine."

" . . . And we took the decision to tell them the whole truth," Dasdahar went on. "Of necessity this included much background information on Untha, the numbers, composition, and inherently nonwarlike nature of the fleet.

181

Their response to this was guarded, and they requested more detailed information. They were particularly interested in the problems met with on the flagship after the Untha-trained personnel had gone into Cold Sleep—"

"Anyone with half a brain," Heglenni put in, "could understand why."

" . . . And now," continued the communications officer quickly, while his eyes pleaded with Heglenni to shut up and not make things more difficult for them, "they have refused to supply any further data about themselves or their race until we agree to certain conditions. One of them is that you, sir, speak with and if possible meet the gas-breather Wah-Lass—"

"No!"

There was a short silence while Heglenni and Dasdahar stared at each other—a hulking, good-natured male who had actually lived on the home world and a sleek, hard female who was nearly always angry and who did not quite believe in the existence of the world on which the other had lived. Then suddenly Gunt was speaking again.

"I do not want to speak to the being Wah-Lass for a reason I will shortly make clear," he said. "Our position here is steadily worsening. More and more reports are coming in of the enemy's depth-bombing their inshore wrecks to keep us from using them as observation posts. As you know, the flagship has been sheltering beside the metal of one of the sunken enemy capital ships, so that our turn must soon come. Consequently we must complete our data on the enemy life-form for earliest possible transmission to the fleet. You will therefore kill the five gas-breathing specimens, making sure that they are not damaged unnecessarily in the process, and transfer them without delay to the flagship so that we can fill the gaps in our knowledge of their physiology."

"No," said Heglenni.

"Is this necessary, sir?" said Dasdahar.

"Unfortunately yes," replied the captain. "I realize that both of you have formed a slight emotional attachment for these beings, that you have the highest admiration for their ability to survive, and that you advocate placing them on the surface to be rescued by their friends.

But they are now in possession of much vital information about us, and if the enemy realized that we were *not* a war fleet they would be less cautious while hunting us and our casualties would be immeasurably greater. I dislike this step as much as you do, but this is war.

"I understand both your feelings," Gunt went on, "and I will overlook your mishandling of the matter as well as your present insubordination. It could also be argued that the specimens would have died anyway if you hadn't discovered them, so you can allay your consciences with the knowledge that—"

"I won't do it!" said Heglenni angrily.

"Neither," said Dasdahar respectfully, "will I."

The verbal explosion which burst from the communicator was followed instants later by a second and greater explosion which smashed against their bodies like some tremendous hammer, obliterating from their minds all thoughts of gas-breathers and insubordination and questions of ethics to leave only a sudden and terrible darkness.

It was a newly discovered wreck lying among rocks in a narrow inlet and this was their first drop on the target; otherwise the drill was very much as before. Drop the bomb, watch a large area of water turn white, try to jump skyward, wait a few minutes for it to settle, and then look for any unusual occurrence. Up to now there had been no unusual occurrences . . .

"God!" said the navigator-bombardier.

"Choppers, para-meds, hover-boats!" the pilot yelled suddenly on the emergency frequency. "Get them here fast! There's people down there, survivors of some kind, floating up! They're in some kind of plastic bag. Some of them . . . I think some of them are still moving!"

XXIV

There were no longer any pockets of gas trapped inside the wreck of *Gulf Trader*, since the shock of the explosion had opened very nearly every seam in her hull, but there was still life. Heglenni and her companion belonged to a species tough both in mind and body, and the compression effects of the depth bomb had been nullified to a certain extent by the compartmented structure of the vessel, not to mention the pockets of gas it had contained which had also helped absorb the shock wave. But the water around the ship lightened and darkened several times before Heglenni was anything like fully conscious, and many more days would pass before her companion would be able to speak properly and move without swimming into things. They were both in considerable pain.

The communicator was undamaged, but subsiding wreckage had cut the line to the outside. As quickly as possible—the heat beams could not be used at full strength in the confined space without their boiling themselves alive—Heglenni cut her way through the roof of what had been Number Ten tank and through to the weather deck. From the opening she could see into the tiny section of corridor and the two small compartments where the gas-breathers had lived before she had extended their quarters. They had been most grateful for the extra living space and Heglenni had been doubly pleased because the transparent bubble had greatly eased the problems of communication. Now all that remained of the extension was a semicircle of hardened sealing compound projecting outwards onto the weather deck to which there adhered tatters of slowly waving plastic. The explosion must have ripped it to shreds and Wah-Lass, and the others, too, of course, with it.

Heglenni felt welling up inside her a pain which had

nothing whatever to do with her many physical injuries, a pain which was a combination of anger and sorrow and helplessness at the inevitability of things.

Self-preservation, the survival of one's self or one's race, was the prime law. Another law was that enemies must be destroyed. Even the enemies themselves agreed on this. But Heglenni had not only been unwilling, she had been unable to kill the gas-breathers in the wreck, and her feelings in the matter had gradually been transmitted to the communications officer. Basically it was a feeling of rebellion against natural and inevitable laws, reinforced by the strange but true fact that Heglenni felt much more understanding and affection for the grotesque, spindly gas-breather Wah-Lass than she did for Captain Gunt. When she looked at the captain she saw a fat, self-confident, highly efficient Unthan who was inclined to be patronizing, when he wasn't being impatient, about her background and manners. But when she looked at Wah-Lass she scarcely saw the gas-breather at all.

Instead she saw a composite picture of the flagship and the face of her father, Deslann Five; and the blind, ravaged features of Hellseggorn of the food ship; and the shadowy faces of all the captains stretching back to the first Deslann. In the picture, too, was the conflict between the Young People and the Seniors, the generations-long war with the food ship, and the over-all suffering which had come in the wake of too much inbreeding and cramped, unnatural surroundings. The technical aptitude which made it possible to survive physically in such hostile surroundings formed only a very small part of the picture in comparison with the sheer, dogged courage and mental discipline which had kept them both going for generation after generation. The flagship had had a purpose in the shape of the target planet and journey's end to give them stability and direction, but the gas-breathers in their wreck had had nothing but the will to survive and to remain as civilized as possible while they were doing it.

Heglenni was glad that it had been their own kind who had killed the gas-breathers. She could not, and would not, have done it.

Moving a short distance from the wreck she found

185

the communications cable and spliced it into the severed lead from the set. She was about to put in a call, wondering if the flagship was at the other end of the line or just another depth-bombed wreck, when there was a sudden disturbance on the surface.

It was a slow-moving area of highly agitated water characteristic of the enemy hover-boats, probably the only kind which could pass over the submerged rocks with safety. The patch of disturbed water slowed and came to a stop almost directly overhead. A large metal object broke through the surface and began to slip down towards her, and Heglenni had a moment of the most horrible kind of fear followed by an angry fatalism. Then she noticed that there was a line attached to the object and stopping it short of the sea bottom, and that it was making loud, distorted, but intelligible noises. . . .

"Captain Heglenni, Captain Gunt, Communicator Dasdahar. Any Unthan person who is in contact with your flagship," it boomed in the slow, labored, and unmistakable accents of the gas-breather Wah-Lass. *"This is a recording of my words, since I am still under the care of the healers, but I can assure you with all truth that my superiors wish for peaceful contact with your race and a nonviolent solution to our problems. A continuing war between us would, as well as bringing about your destruction as a civilized race, so poison our oceans and our gas envelope with radioactive material that our own species might be lethally affected.*

"Until now we had thought that our destruction of the ships in the vanguard of your fleet had committed us irrevocably to war as the only solution possible, but now that we know that the ships destroyed contained only food animals, peace is still possible between us.

"The remaining units of your fleet will arrive ten days from now. We will not oppose their landing, but urge that you signal us before then so that we will know that you do in fact desire peace. . . ."

It was at that point that Heglenni succeeded in getting through to the flagship. She said quickly, "Heglenni and Dasdahar here, sir. We were injured when the gas-breathers depth-bombed their wreck. I don't know how long exactly we have been unconscious, but there have been new developments. Listen, sir!"

"No need, Heglenni," the captain replied, his voice distorted both by distance and deep emotion. "They've had one of those gadgets dangling above our heads here for the best part of a day. We are signaling them now in the manner they have suggested and we will transmit the good news to the rest of the fleet.

"This is the answer, Heglenni. I think there is going to be peace."

. .

"Thousands of Unthan ships landing in all the oceans of the world," said the officer wearing the spectacles, "and all we could see from the headland was what looked like three slow-moving shooting stars. It was a bit of an anti-climax."

Smiling, the admiral said, "He's right, Surgeon Commander. You didn't miss a thing."

Wallis looked at them without speaking. The one with the glasses was standing almost at attention beside the bed while the older one was lying across it with his weight propped on one elbow. Behind them were the red walls, ceiling, and floor which had been painted to represent rust-streaked bulkheads and the tank of tropical fish set flush with the wall in a window frame, all designed to make him feel at home. The real windows had been painted over and his only view of the outside came to him via the TV, which for some odd reason did not bring on his agoraphobia. His bed was so warm and so comfortable and so fantastically, unbelievably dry that he did not feel at home in it at all—it felt more like Heaven. There were times—the present moment, in fact—when he did not feel in contact with his surroundings at all.

One of the doctors had told him that the feeling was nothing to worry about, being due simply to massive doses of medication and the aftermath of double pneumonia, severe malnutrition, exposure, decompression, and shock through being blown to the surface by a depth charge, and that he was lucky to be alive.

"It's a case of a big fleet landing in an enormous ocean," said the officer with the glasses. "You know, if

187

they'd landed three or four centuries ago we might have put it down to a meteor shower and not even realized they were there. Now, however, we know they are there and vice versa. Our people are beginning to accept the idea of their being refugees rather than an invading force. But it is an extremely tenuous image. Can we really trust them not to—"

"You can trust them," said Wallis sharply.

"Of course, Commander," the other said placatingly. "They're friends of yours so you should know. But what I was going to say was can we trust them not to boob and spoil things? Certainly we have oceans enough to spare so far as living space goes, and they'll be able to help us farm the seas more efficiently, thus helping relieve our food problems. There is a lot we can learn from them about spaceship design and power plants, the Cold Sleep they've developed, and undersea technology in general. And the learning process will be two-way; there'll be progress in all areas of knowledge. It wouldn't surprise me if we can go to the stars before too long, and not by putting ourselves into cold storage for a couple of centuries, either.

"But the point I'm trying to make," he went on excitedly, "is that there is bound to be friction between us as well as cooperation. Their life-span, for instance, is much shorter than ours. A couple of centuries from now the seas may be overpopulated as well as the land. There are bound to be incidents, accidents, where humans or Unthans are injured or killed. What I'm getting at is that we must make the widest possible contact with them *now,* so that in the future these incidents will seem less important!"

"What he's really getting at, Commander," said the admiral drily, "is when are you going to stop malingering in bed and go to work? Every Unthan message we've received—and your young people have translated quite a few for us—has asked how Wah-Lass is doing. They seem to like you as well as trust you, for some odd reason. How did you do it?"

Wallis already knew that he was to be the human ambassador to the Unthans on earth, that he would probably spend the rest of his life living under the sea and talking to Heglenni and Gunt and the others and teaching members of his own race to talk to them, too. He knew it and accepted it. In fact, the truth was that he was horribly afraid of the open sky and the tall buildings and trees, which always seemed to be about to fall on him. Unlike the young people who had survived and who seemed more able to adapt, Wallis was going back to the sea bed. But this time, the admiral had assured him, he would be as warm and dry and well fed as he was here in the Naval hospital.

And he knew that the admiral and the Army officer with the glasses were not criticizing him in any way, that they were deeply concerned for him and that their respect for him was quite embarrassing—Wallis had listened to too many people talking in absolute darkness for him to be mistaken in a tone of voice. The question about malingering was simply a pleasantry and the second . . . well, how *had* he done it?

"We had something in common," said Wallis. "Both our ships were at sea for a long, long time. . . ."

*The publisher of the best science fiction in
the world presents*

JAMES WHITE

1972 SELECTIONS FROM
THE PUBLISHER OF THE BEST
SCIENCE FICTION IN THE WORLD

1971 SELECTIONS FROM THE PUBLISHER OF THE BEST SCIENCE FICTION IN THE WORLD